COMMAND PERFORMANCE

NATHAN VANHORN'S SERVICE TO COUNTRY DURING THE AMERICAN CIVIL WAR

BOOK I

as transcribed by

P. J. Wright

pjwrght@aol.com

Ὑπό Τῷ Ἥλιῷ

HYPO TO HELIO BOOKS

Houston

Paperback ISBN: 978-1-938293-16-0
Ebook ISBN: 978-1-938293-17-7

The front-cover photograph is of the *USS Saint Louis* (a.k.a. *USS Baron DeKalb*). The flag on the stern of the ship is not historical.

Front-cover render art by: P. J. Wright

Civil War fonts are licensed from WaldenFont.

Contact the author at: pjwrght AT aol DOT com

BISAC Subject Headings:
Fic006000—Fiction > Thrillers > Espionage
Fic011000—Fiction > Gay
Fic014000—Fiction > Historical
His036050—History > United States > Civil War period
Per001000—Performing Arts > Acting & Auditioning
Per011020—Performing Arts > Theater > History & Criticism

HYPO TO HELIO BOOKS, 2427 Clearbrook Dr., Missouri City, TX, 77489-6061

I.
The Early Years

That the reader may most fully understand the how and why of my career as a spy in the service of the Federal cause in that lamentable conflagration which most recently tore this great nation asunder, I think it beneficial for me to set down a brief history of my early years and my career in the theater.

I was born to Joshua and Charity VanHorn on December 18th, in the year of our Lord 1837, in the city of New Haven, Connecticut.

I was one of twins. Therein lies much, I think, of my nature, and much that bears on the tale I will soon tell. My sister Elizabeth was born but a brief span of minutes after my own squalling arrival upon this Earth. It is a rarity of nature, or so I am told, for fraternal twins to be born one male and one female. Experts tell me the odds of that are upon the order of one in any hundred.

Liz and I were much alike in feature and form—both blessed with sky-blue eyes—though we were much disparate in temperament. Liz was ever the dutiful, obedient child, always Father's favorite before his untimely departure from this life when we were but nine years of age. I, on the other hand, was quite the rapscallion. My own memories of Father often feature a none-too-sparing acquaintance with his widest leather belt. In his defense I must say that more often than not, the chastisement was well deserved.

Lest I give the unwarranted impression that my tender years were nothing but misery and mistreatment, it must be clearly understood that my Father's household was a happy one. His profession as a lecturer of philosophy and humanities at the University saw us well provided and wanting for none of the material comforts. In addition, Mother's family (the Currands of Massachusetts) is, as you no doubt know, of old and venerable stock, to say nothing of impressive wealth and social connection.

No, my early years should have been as blissful and carefree as those of any of my contemporaries. "Should have been" but for the trick that conspiring Dame Fortune and Mother Nature had played upon me.

As I have stated, Liz and I were much alike in form and feature. Sadly for me, the form and feature were very much Mother's.

For Liz, this was a blessing. More and more these days, I see in her lovely countenance the striking beauty that was our Mother.

For me, a young lad growing up amongst rambunctious peers, it was a curse most cutting. Ever were the taunts of "sissy" and "milksop" ringing in my ears. Nor did my slender frame or my short stature, which never topped the height of five feet one inch, serve to my defense on those occasions when I could endure the taunts no longer, and I sought physical remedy from my tormentors.

Perhaps, if Father had been spared, I would have learned more masculine recourse. But pneumonia robbed me both of father and opportunity in the winter of 1846.

My tutelage and my formation therefore devolved upon Mother. I do not regret that. Never should it be thought otherwise. As I say, my formative years were happy ones, there in the company of Mother and Liz.

It might be assumed that I lacked entirely for virile influence and nurturing, but this was not the case. I was not raised in the model of womankind, for all that I would have physically fit the role. No, Mother was wise in this and saw to it that I had suitable masculine companionship, both contemporary and adult. I have such share of boyhood romps and masculine adventures and initiations as any callow youth can boast.

Still, there were rainy afternoons when there were no males available for companionship, when Mother and Liz and I passed the hours in feminine occupation.

Here, I would be less than unabbreviated and would do disservice to my narrative, if I did not mention that upon diverse occasion we amused ourselves by engaging in a little fantasy play in which I enacted the role of "Corinne," the name chosen for me had my gender matched that of my twin. I was never loathe in this, and took as great a delight in enacting the part and costume as Mother and Liz took for the masquerade's support.

Ever have flights of fancy and imaginative discourse been my delight.

Yet all of this does not bring me closer to my tale of my service to Cause and Country. It but sets the foundation for the narrative. For the true beginnings of that tale, we must return to the summer of my thirteenth year.

Mother was very bohemian in outlook, and lively in her appetites. Her greatest joy was attendance upon the many plays and operas available in that very cosmopolitan city, New Haven. Quickly Liz and I learned to cultivate our Mother's passion for the performing arts.

It was while attending one of these performances, when I was feeling the first stirrings of my male nature, the event occurred that would forever set the course of my life.

To this day, I do not know the opera being performed. I was still naive about such matters, not yet possessing what I modestly confess to be an extensive knowledge of classical opera. I vividly remember the ingénue of the piece, however. She was, to my young eyes, a golden haired goddess— beautiful—virginal. Desirable in ways that my yet nascent masculinity could only begin to comprehend. I sat transfixed whenever she occupied the stage. Her voice was soprano; her role, that of the tragic maiden doomed forever to yearn for, yet never attain, the arms of her heroic lover. That image lingers in my mind, as clear today as on that magical night when first I beheld who still for me is the icon of womanhood.

When the performance was ended, I sat enthralled in my seat, high up in Mother's box, as she entertained various acquaintances calling upon us. I paid little heed to the adult conversation droning on in the background, my mind aflame with the image of my unattainable paramour.

That is, until I heard the mention of the character's name together with praise for the artistry of *il castrato*, and the bemoaning of the gradual disappearance of that art form. I spun in my seat and with youthful exuberance thrust myself into the conversation.

"*Il castrato?* What is that?"

I remember the speaker, fittingly enough, was a doctor of Mother's acquaintance, a lecturer in human anatomy at the University. "Why Nathan, that is a man who has chosen to forsake his masculinity in favor of the ability to perform such roles as you just witnessed. It is a classical form dating—"

"A *man?* Do you mean to say that *she was a man?*"

There were smiles at my obvious astonishment and innocent naïveté. Perhaps it was with memory of our "fantasy play" that Mother, a slight tease in her voice, asked, "But wasn't he lovely, Nathan? Wasn't his voice angelic?"

I would have understanding of this impossibility, so I ignored her and still demanded of the doctor, "But how? How is it done?"

Which, of course, turned the indulgent smiles to incipient embarrassment and fluster. I don't remember how the subject was escaped, only that it was, for it was several years before I had full understanding.

But understanding or not, that fascination, like the little acorn, had been planted in my psyche. It flourished and grew, in time becoming a spreading, mind-filling oak. The artistry, the imagination, the ability to live so many lives, to be so many things, took me. From that night forward, my life upon the stage was a foregone conclusion.

In this, the choice of the theater as my life, I think Dame Fortune made redress for the cruel trick she had perpetrated upon me in her choice for my physical form. Unlike so many families of that era, we were comfortable in the material sense. There was never need for me to toil for my daily bread. There was money, and sufficient, to last me a dozen lifetimes. I therefore had the leisure to pursue whatever course suited my fancy. That Mother was the woman she was, with such forward thinking outlook, also aided me in my resolution. I don't doubt but that she wished for me a more stable and, we must be honest, socially acceptable lifestyle. Yet I think that in her heart of hearts she understood how my nature and formative years had molded me. If she ever regretted or begrudged me my choice, she never gave hint of it. Indeed, the only recrimination I ever received was from gentle Liz who, on occasion, would look me in the eye and in mild tones reproof me with "Oh Nate, what would Father say?"

Yet I cared little. My feet were firmly set upon the road of footlight and greasepaint.

I wish it could be said that I attained vast acclaim and fortune in my thespian endeavor in New Haven. Candor and modesty deny me this. In masculine roles, my only noteworthy reviews were when playing juvenile characters. It was in feminine guise that I attained my greatest successes. Then the reviews were often rave.

Still, I am not so deceived as to believe it was as much for my skill at feminine personation, (though, as will be seen, that skill was laudable,) as it was for the novelty of my ability. Time and again, the words "uncanny verisimilitude to femininity" and "the very image of womanhood" appeared in my mentions.

I suppose I now and then wished for recognition of my thespian talent, to receive acclaim as a great actor. Still, in all, I was content.

I moved within a polite, if somewhat avant-garde society. Often I attended functions (at the host's request) *en femme*. This, much to the delight of those "in the know," and the discomfit of those at first in ignorance. I confess a guilty pleasure at the many charming beaus whose admiration and desire I enflamed, only to see it dashed when whispered confidence of my true nature finally reached their ears. I excuse it as the pride of an artisan in a work of art well executed. Nor did I ever, in good conscience, believe I caused lasting harm with my masquerade. Certainly, I never took any actions that I intended truly hurtful.

The years passed. My fame, if never of that status that evokes world renown, was sufficient to sustain my pride. I had reached that point in my career and maturation when I could play any role offered me.

My stature, my thin, slow-growing beard, my soft-featured face, my light, airy voice whose timber and pitch I could control through an astonishing variety of range; these allowed me to attempt and succeed at anything from juvenile male through ingénue to regal dame. With the sleight of hand that my extensive knowledge of makeup afforded me, and with some concentration on my vocalization, I could also play the male bravo—albeit a bravo short of stature.

I became much sought after by the producers of theatrical productions for the yeoman service I could perform. I was well liked and respected within the professional circles of my orbit.

Then came the Great War of Secession. Upon a night that lives still in my memory, there occurred an event that altered my comfortable, familiar world in the twinkle of an eye.

II.
A Role to Die For

I would be disingenuous if I stated that the War, at first, much occupied my thoughts. It seemed to me a distant, alien conflagration, no more bearing upon me than some war in Europe. My politics were, for the most part, nonexistent. I know that I occasionally read the editorials that alternately castigated or lauded (depending upon the city of their publication) the exploits of the various characters from the early years, before open conflict erupted.

I noticed that the topic of conversations at the many soirees I attended concerned, more and more, the fundamental necessity for State's Rights or the monstrous evil that was Slavery. To my shame, I admit: Were I in masculine guise, I would attempt to steer the conversation to more light hearted topics: gaming or literature. If my guise were at the time feminine, I'm even more ashamed to confess my response was almost always a light, unconcerned giggle, a flutter of my fan, and a pouting "Oh, all this is so far beyond me—and so *boring*." It embarrasses me to confess that, my assumed feminine charms being what they were, it was a simple trick for me to then guide the conversation to whatever topic I wished.

It should have been a clue to me that if my partners in conversation were women, the topic remained fixed upon the more serious, and I quickly found myself excluded.

In those days, to my deep remorse, my thoughts were shallow and unconcerned with events transpiring in the World without. More shamefully, when the great bloodletting began in earnest, my chief notice of it was through the decrease in the frequency of merrymaking, and a more somber tone to those gatherings to which I was invited.

The change came one night in my dressing room after an unmemorable performance.

****

Our troupe, renowned in New Haven, was at that time performing the Molière comedy *A School for Scandal.* I had the role of Mistress Snake, and was performing it nightly with great gusto. Upon completion of the performance, and after the obligatory meeting with the many admirers who had ventured backstage to greet the artists, I had retired to my dressing room to remove my elaborate costume and makeup. There was to be a post-performance party at one of my confidant's homes, and I was eager to be on my way.

I had just doffed the intricately coifed wig, and was beginning to remove the heavy greasepaint that made my features expressive in the harsh glare of the limelighting, when there came a gentle tap at my door.

"Come in," said I. I was expecting either one of the theater lackeys with some trivial message, or a charming actress of my acquaintance with an offer of companionship to the party. (I had determined to go in my masculine guise that evening, the portrayal of Mistress Snake providing surfeit for any feminine urgings I may have entertained.)

To my surprise, my visitor was a stranger to me. He was tall, approaching six feet in height, with well-formed, ruggedly handsome features and piercing blue eyes.

He showed himself a gentleman of quality when he quickly took color upon his cheeks and averted his gaze. In order to remove the artfully conceived highlight and shadow applied for the creation of my "bosom", (this being necessitated by the deep-plunging décolletage of the Restoration gown that I wore,) I had unfastened the first four buttons of said garment. The opening of the door found me industriously rubbing that region with a chamois.

"Oh, I beg your pardon." He quickly made to absent himself from my boudoir, but I stopped him with an airy chuckle.

"I take it as great compliment that my characterization was of such quality that you'd grant me a maiden's modesty. Please, sir, come in."

My reward was a rueful grin and the offer of his card.

I read "Jacob Niles, Esq." and a fashionable address in the College Quarter. Thinking my visitor simply another fan, and wishing to be on my way to the party, I made no offer of a seat but merely smiled, set his card aside, and asked, "To what do I owe the pleasure of this visit, sir?"

At first he seemed to be just what I had taken him for, when he began, "I much enjoyed your performance tonight. All your ensemble gave great life and honesty to the roles portrayed."

I nodded and continued to smile. "You are most kind to say so."

Then, without invitation, he closed the door and stepped farther into the room. "I wonder, do you find the personification of women to be easier when the part is laid out for you?"

I was a bit nonplused by his forwardness, but the question itself was one I'd heard before. "No. I find rather the opposite. For me, the roles come more alive when the invention of the character is my own. To that end, I think every good performer creates the role anew with each performance."

My guest smiled, as though I'd just provided him with intelligence he had hoped to obtain. "So, you would say that a good actor can invent a role *ex tempore?* That is to say, without the need for framework or prior planning?"

I nodded and confirmed it was my belief that an actor without quick and deft imagination was, at best, a mere 'technician' and not a true artist.

Again my guest apparently found this assertion agreeable, for again I was rewarded with a smile. "I confess a limited knowledge of matters theatrical, but I suspected that it would be thus."

My unease was growing, and instead of helping this rather peculiar conversation along, I simply regarded my guest with a neutral expression. Frankly, I hoped to convey a hint that he was rapidly losing my interest; and that his company, though initially welcome, was failing of its attraction.

His next words caught me completely off guard. "What is your position on the question of Secession?"

There was no subtlety in my reply. "And what concern is that of yours?"

Now, again without invitation, he sat in a chair beside the racks upon which hung my many costumes. "It concerns me deeply, as I think it would concern anyone of good conscience."

I stood, with the intention of making my anger at the implied slur readily evident. Such are the vicissitudes of my fate that a man, dishabille in a satin gown, makes poor show of bluster and threat. "Sir, I think you should leave."

But he simply sat there, that smile playing around his lips. "Shall I understand that you hold no strong position either way on that question?"

"You are d____d impudent! I feel no great compulsion to reply to a rascal who thrusts himself into my company solely for the purpose of asking boorish questions. You will leave—Now!"

For emphasis, I raised my right arm and pointed to the door. In a turn befitting the farce I had just recently enacted, the bodice of my gown, already loosened, decided at that moment to begin a slow slide down my chest. I was, perforce, compelled to gather it in my left arm and press it against that self-same "bosom". Needless to say, my intended show of threat was far less intimidating than intended. Indeed, I could not have seemed less threatening had I played it so.

My tormentor only smiled more broadly. "Do you consider yourself loyal to your country? I would assume, being of an honorable and long-established Yankee family, that you consider yourself to be a citizen of the United States, rather than the Confederacy."

"Again, sir, your questions are offensive in the extreme. I will not dignify them with an answer. Leave."

Still he made no move to comply. "Does it bother you to know, as we sit here after a genuinely delightful evening of fantasy and play, that there are men preparing for the morrow in some lonely place, far from home and family? Does it disturb you to know that they are dreading a coming battle where, most likely, more than one of them will give their lives to preserve the Union and advance the cause of Abolition, while you don makeup and prepare for lighthearted entertainment?"

I sneered in return. "You make your own sentiments well known, that I will say for you."

He nodded, the smile now gone and his features grown grave and serious. "Yes, I would think my sentiments were clear. I make no apology for them, for I think them honorable. And I ask you again, sir, where do your sentiments lie?"

Believing that the only way to be rid of this crass fellow was to give him some answer, I replied, "Well, since you seem determined to make it your business, I will tell you. Yes, I do consider myself a Unionist. Yes, I do oppose slavery as a great evil. And yes, I do concern myself with the welfare of those souls brave enough to lay down their all for what they believe is right—provided their cause is just. Does this give you satisfaction? Will you now do me the courtesy to leave?"

Still no movement from my infuriating, unshakable inquisitor.

"And how shall you give form to your sentiments? What shall you do to advance your beliefs?"

This was growing intolerable. "You have overstepped, sir. You will be gone instantly, or I will summon assistance and evict you!"

Ignoring my threat, his face assumed a calculating aspect. "Or perhaps, appeal to your patriotism is the wrong tack. Let me ask you this: What would you give to play a role, the likes of which have never before been attempted? A role that will require of you all your skill and talent? A role that, when completed, will have your name the topic of conversation for years to come? Does that interest you?"

Have I spoken of shame? Here now is my greatest: Where appeals to noble sentiments of patriotism and valor left me unmoved, an invocation of my overweening pride at last caught my interest.

"*What?* Shall I be given to understand all this was prelude to the offer of a role?"

A nod and a smile. "Just so, if you should choose to view it as such. And as I say, a role requiring such unique talent and consummate skill that we have decided that you alone can undertake it with success."

Let it never be said that I am slow of comprehension. The preamble to this offer, the tenor of my visitor's early statements, the unforgettable nearness of the War and all the dangers and intrigues it presented, quickly coalesced within my thought and I could guess what was hinted at here.

"You are from the Government, are you not? And do I not rightly guess that you wish me to undertake some impersonation in the furtherance of the Union's cause? Might I not even guess that this impersonation would make use of my talents at feminine characterization?"

To which, my interrogator only smiled and nodded.

****

The next morning found me in attendance upon my new associate Mr. Niles at his offices near the Old Arsenal building. I was conservatively attired, in one of my finer frock coats with matching trousers and a newly tailored linen shirt with cravat.

He had demurred of any further discourse there at the theater, insisting instead that if I wished more acquaintance with the matter he proposed, I must present myself to the progenitor of the whole scheme for his inspection and approval.

My motives for pursuing this endeavor are, to me, still something of a mystery. I would like to say that Niles's invocation of the hardships and travail that so many good men suffered on my behalf, whether or not I knew or cared of it, had awakened something of my long-slumbering conscience. This may be so. But my curiosity over the proposed work, the delicious intrigue and opportunity to employ my talents in such a unique and challenging venue—surely this was strong motivation as well.

In any event, ten o'clock found me standing before a nondescript if genteel brownstone near the heart of the city. I remember feeling a moment's hesitation and a small stab of something very akin to stage fright, (an emotion long unfamiliar to me,) before I mounted the steps bound for Niles' suite of rooms and my rendezvous with destiny.

The building was a collection of private offices grouped around a central clerk's area, wherein a pool of shared secretaries—all busy young men—labored on behalf of all the professionals inhabiting the space. I stood uncertainly for a moment, until a secretary seated near me noticed my apparent indecision when he glanced up.

"May I be of assistance, sir?" he inquired in polite tones.

"If you would, please." I handed him my card, then continued, "I have an appointment with Mr. Niles. Is his office one of these?"

The young man glanced at my card. "Ah, Mr. VanHorn. Indeed, you have found your destination. You are expected, sir. If you would step this way?"

I complied, and was led to a doorway communicating with the rear of the secretarial area. My guide knocked once, opened the door, and announced me. Then he stepped aside, motioning me within.

I found the room to be well appointed with several wing chair of sumptuous brown leather, a large, imposing desk, and walls lined with treatises on law and (what I presume were) digests of case decisions.

Seated behind the desk was a positively patrician gentleman of late middle age with steel gray hair, and he was fiercely mustachioed in the bristling, "grandee" style that has recently become the fashion. Across the desk from him and to his left, Niles, dressed in a natty gray flannel suit, rose at my entrance.

Before Niles could even begin proper introductions, the old gentleman *harrumph*ed once and grumbled, "So. This is the actor, is it? Small fellow—not all that effeminate. You say he can pull off this bogus?"

As Niles made to shake my hand, I wondered if I'd made some kind of blunder. There had been no command for me to accouter myself in woman's guise, and frankly, it had not occurred to me to do so. It was my expectation that this was to be a business meeting, and that solemnity and probity were to be the order of the day.

Niles pumped my hand just as if we were old friends. "Oh, no fear of that. Mr. Nathan VanHorn, may I introduce Captain Silas Wickman? Captain Wickman, Mr. VanHorn."

I moved to shake the old gentleman's hand. "Your servant, sir."

He only glowered at me. "Don't have much confidence in this scheme, not much confidence at all."

The awkward moment stretched until Niles motioned me to the other chair. "Well, that is the first reason for this meeting, isn't it, sir? To see if confidence might be built."

As I seated myself, Wickman treated me to another *harrumph*.

In the ensuing silence, I had the distinct sense that I was being judged for fitness; though what the criterion was, remained obscure. I determined to take the initiative. "Gentlemen, perhaps it would be well to advise me, before the matter proceeds further, just what this 'scheme' is? Surely, that would be a basis for beginning, would it not?"

Wickman turned that piercing gaze on Niles. "You didn't tell him what it was all about?"

Niles shrugged. "I thought it wiser to leave that until we had settled upon him as the choice."

" 'Choice'? Not many other candidates for the job, I'd say. Might as well tell him. If he can't carry it off, won't be any more of this, and the whole scheme will be for nothing anyway. As I see it, it's him or not at all." Then I was again the object of scrutiny. "Not that I think it's to be him, mind you."

It was uncomfortable sitting there, having that conversation proceed above my head and I was becoming a bit short. "Again I must ask, what scheme do you propose?"

Niles turned to me. "You had the gist of it last night. In simplest terms, we propose an expedition of espionage into the very heart of the Confederacy. We wish you to undertake this expedition, making full use of your talents to appear in many guises, both masculine and feminine. At heart, it's really just that simple."

Wickman interjected with "Simple—*humph*—so is falling off a cliff."

Niles tried to hide his annoyance at the lack of help he was getting from his presumed superior.

"But for whom am I to undertake this expedition, should I choose to proceed? Who are you? Whom do you represent?"

My two companions exchanged a glance. Then Niles, in a rather tentative fashion, replied, "Well—that is a bit of a difficult question. You may assume that this is a sanctioned affair. That is to say, approved by the Government, but, er. . ."

The sudden coyness supplied the answer. "But it is not an enterprise that anyone of high office wishes to be identified with. Do I guess correctly?"

Niles was struggling for a reply when Wickman snorted, "Would you want your name to get tacked on to this if you had to run for re-election in a few years?"

I smiled and shook my head. "No. Even without full intelligence of the plan, I think not. Still, I need at least some assurance of its legitimacy before I can commit to it."

Niles sighed. "But therein is the difficulty. We are prepared to offer such assurance, but only to the person who agrees to undertake the effort. I fear there is nothing for it, but for you to act on trust. The initial commitment must be so based."

Ever have I been a bit of scoundrel. I have the memory of Father's belt to bolster that statement. And surely one who makes his life upon the stage can boast he doesn't usually faint of new and unusual circumstance. I nodded to Niles; then to the Captain, I said, "Well then, I shall depend upon your trust. I shall agree to undertake this endeavor, if I feel it is within my scope."

Niles was grinning with unrestrained enthusiasm. "Good for you, sir! Your trust is not misplaced."

I looked from face to face. There was a pause. "So, gentlemen, the proof?"

Niles turned to Wickman who, with yet another snort, opened a pasteboard folder lying at his right hand. From it, he withdrew a single sheet of paper. This he spun around so it would be legible to me, then slid it toward me across the desk.

I had to rise and stand across from him to read it. Throughout my inspection, Wickman kept two fingers upon the document, apparently mistrustful that I would try to snatch it away.

I quickly skimmed the text, which seemed to be an ambiguously worded commission to carry out "acts and plans for the continued furtherance of the war effort." In short, it used a good deal of words to convey little meaning. The document was unimpressive until I reached the signature at the end. I admit I gasped.

"*Him?* He is the author of this undertaking?"

Wickman offered me my first smile, albeit a small, sour one. "Why does that surprise you? Surely you know he loves the theater. Loves his games and jests too. Just like him to come up with something like this."

The paper was quickly returned to its folder and the folder was then secured within a locked drawer in the desk. I was quite dumbfounded. I had thought this some small assay by a few individuals in some little department of the Army. I had no idea of the heights from which the idea had descended.

"Gentlemen, you may take it that I am sufficiently impressed with the legitimacy of your cause."

Wickman surprised me by snapping his fingers and growling to Niles. "You see why it'll never work? He's far too gullible. Takes folks at their word. Won't do, Niles, won't do."

My confusion must have been writ large across my face, for without my asking, a troubled Niles shook his head and said to me, "How do you know that document was genuine?"

I spluttered for a moment. "Why—But you offered it to me in good faith. Surely—"

Wickman leaned forward, both hands flat on the desk before him. "Lies, boy! Cheats and deceptions! Misleading folks for your own wicked ends. That's the bread and butter of this kind of work. In the world you're suddenly so willing to enter, nobody tells you a truth when a lie will suffice."

"Then how am I to proceed? How am I to know what to think?"

Niles again: "What does your heart tell you? That must ever be your guide, Nathan. That and your judgment of the person with whom you deal."

I sat back in my chair and thought about it for a long time, as the other two watched my face.

There is a talent of actors not much discoursed upon. It is our stock and trade to create believable individuals from the whole cloth of our imagination. To build a thing, you must understand a thing. So it is with our artistic creations. It is from our study of people that we gain our ability to mimic them. I think this makes us good judges of motive and character.

I judged these two to be more than they seemed. And both of them, I also judged, were dedicated to a cause that I somehow *felt* to be right.

At length, I nodded. "Gentlemen, I confess I am not native to this world of which you speak. But I can carry off a deception with the best of them. Of that, Mr. Niles at least has good proof. For the rest—well, I'm nothing if not a quick study."

Niles turned to Wickman. "Please, sir. I think he is the one for the job. You know as well as I how many of the skills that sustain this work are learned. I assure you, I think Mr. VanHorn an apt and fitting—"

Wickman waved a hand. "No doubt, no doubt. Never said he wasn't a likely fellow. But still, I just don't see this whole scheme as workable. Don't see it. Smoke and mirrors and play-acting—"

Niles continued to press his case. "If you could but see him in portrayal—"

I interjected, "But that is easily arranged."

Wickman would have none of it. "Theater make-believe is one thing. Don't doubt but that you're good at it. Seen the papers that say so. But this is real, what we're discussing. No scripts for this, you know. Not at all the same thing."

I smiled. "Let me propose this. How stands your schedule for the enactment of this plan?"

They exchanged a glance, then Niles allowed, "We are but in the formative stages. Why?"

"Is there time for a leisurely proof of my ability?"

Another exchange of looks. Wickman asked, "What do you mean?"

Instead of answering his question, I rephrased my earlier question: "Have we a week within which I might operate to demonstrate my skills?"

They were, by now, both showing signs of uncertainty and confusion. After a moment's mutual consideration, Niles offered a tentative, "I think we've a week, surely, before the plans must be more fully developed. What say you, Captain? Shall we take this offer of demonstration?"

Wickman eyed me narrowly. "Just what kind of proof do you propose?"

Now it was my turn for an enigmatic smile. "Why, leave that to me."

III.
Exercises in Mischief

At first, I had never intended for my "proof" to require more than one day.

However, in my career as scoundrel alluded to before, I had learned that a deception is the better carried off when unexpected. Therefore, I had no further intercourse with either Niles or the Captain for the following two days. Rather, I simply used my theatrically acquired skills at dissembling to don inconspicuous guise, sometimes male, sometimes female, and observed my quarry from a distance.

I was overjoyed to see that despite their profession of moving within a world much clandestine and mysterious, the Captain was a rather prosaic fellow of very predictable habit. He rose promptly at seven o'clock each day. He broke his fast at seven–thirty, then strolled at a leisurely pace to his club, arriving punctually at the stroke of nine. There he spent the remainder of the morning in converse with his club mates. Luncheon was ever at half past noon at either Carmody's or at The Greens.

In the afternoon, business affairs took him about the city in an unpredictable pattern. I quickly determined that there was no fruitful access to be gained there. Nor did I see much chance of accosting him at his home during evenings, for he was a rather solitary old bachelor, and not much given to entertaining.

However, I did find opportunity for what I hoped would be my masterstroke, on the second day of my reconnoiter. I had been following Wickman down the street in the guise of a common working man, my Irish cloth cap pulled low over brows sufficiently darkened with the application of crepe-hair brows—brows that matched my now hirsute cheeks and chin—when I observed him to enter a laundering establishment on Harbor Street. Slouching near the door, I overheard him to inquire about the readiness of his tail coat for a party he was to attend at Justice Blanford's residence this coming Thursday (two days hence). Receiving assurance that all would be in readiness in ample time, the proprietor received one of the good Captain's *harrumph*s as that worthy was almost out the door.

I could not have wished for a better chance. The Justice was an old family friend of my Mother's, and something of an aficionado of my thespian career. I was certain that he would think it quite the jest to act in my aid.

But before my masterwork, I assayed a few "pen and ink sketches" that I relate to you thus:

****

Item: Wednesday morning (the third day after my initial briefing with Niles and Captain Wickman) finds the Captain well en route to his club when he chances upon a small, elderly woman in bombazine and heavy veil, her halting progress down the boardwalk heavily dependent upon a gnarled hickory cane. Just as the Captain draws abreast of her, she apparently finds need to cross the busy thoroughfare, beside which the two of them are proceeding.

Twice she attempts the crossing; twice is she frustrated by the volume of traffic, and her own decrepitude and obvious dependence upon the aid of her cane.

The Captain, a gentleman, promptly accosts the old woman. "Madam. Wish to cross, do you?"

Twinkling eyes regard him from beneath the obscuring veil. "Aye, laddie. Sure and I do! But di'vil the hurley-burley!"

The Captain offers his arm. "Happens I'm bound for the other side myself. Allow me."

The old crone gratefully accepts his offer and they make somewhat halting, (and with the rapid advance of the various horses and carriages, more than somewhat harrowing!) progress. All the while, the old woman regales the Captain with her recollection of the more genteel times of her youth in Dublin when such bustle was never to be seen. "Ah sure, an' what's the world comin' to, I wonder!"

****

Item: As the good Captain leaves his club that self-same afternoon, upon the corner northwest from the entrance, he chances upon a very scruffy and ill-clothed boy watching the various gentlefolk pass.

No sooner has the Captain approached within hail than the lad solicits him, one grimy hand outstretched.

"Please, sir, spare a penny?"

The Captain regards the wretch with disdain. "What, boy? Do you think I'll give you a coin simply for the asking?"

The child looks up with huge, beseeching eyes. "Please, sir. It's for my Ma, you understand. She—she's doin' poorly."

"And what of your father, eh? Isn't that his affair? Isn't it his affair to see you're not out upon the streets as a common beggar? What of him, eh?"

"My Pa, sir? He were kilt in the War. Kilt dead at Bull Run he were, bearin' the Colors fer the Third Connecticut!"

"Eh? Killed in the War, you say?"

A proud nod and a squaring of shoulders that were too slender for the burden they sought to carry.

"And how old are you, boy?"

The answer is a defiant "Thirteen, sir."

"*How* old?"

"Well—thirteen come next September. Please, sir. It's been a while since Ma et that good, and she's awful poorly."

The Captain's tone becomes, if possible, more gruff than normal. "Well, I don't hold with beggary, I surely don't. But here." He pulls something from the pocket of his vest. "Now you take that to the address that's on there. Can you read? Good. Well, just see that you're there at seven tomorrow morning. Sharp on the hour, boy. Ask for O'Donnal. Tell him the Captain said to find some work for you. You might mention your Momma's state to him too."

The lad stares at the card as though it is the Keys to the Kingdom. "Oh, sir! I'll be there sharp! You can bet on it!"

The old gentleman grumbles, "See that you are." Then more fishing in his vest pocket produces a silver dollar. "Count that an advance upon your wages. Now, be off with you!"

Since the Captain has quickly turned and walked away, one might wonder if he believes the boy doesn't see the small, gentle smile his "God bless you, sir! Thank you, sir!" provokes.

****

Item: The Captain, arriving the next morning at his Club upon his usual hour.

A well-dressed dandy in a bowler hat approaches and accosts the Captain with "*Sprechen Sie Deutsch, mein guter Herr?*"

The Captain regards this mustachioed stranger. "Eh? What's that? What did you say?"

The reply is a far more tentative, "Er—*Ist* you *das* German *gesprechen?*"

The Captain's reply is a stare of obvious incomprehension writ large across his features.

Realizing the answer to his question about the Captain's fluency in German, the little fellow tries a different tack. Laying a hand on the Captain's arm, he inquires, "*Bitte, mein Herr—was ist* a clock?"

The Captain's response to this new avenue of approach is to scowl at the clearly unwelcome hand on his arm.

But the little dandy is persistent. " 'A clock.' *Was ist* a clock?"

"Are you quite mad, sir?"

"*Himmel!* I make der question, *Wie Spät ist es?* Vere on der clock—Ach! D__n der English!"

The good Captain rears back in affront. "The duce you say!"

Apparently finally realizing that he is giving unintended offense, the little fellow waves his hands in frustration. "*Nein, nein!* I *ist* sorry on you. Mine English—they are not so goot. *Bitte, was ist die*—time? *Die* time? *Ja?*"

"Ah! 'What is the time?' *Humph*, you might have said that in the first place." The Captain pulls an ornate pocket watch from his vest and squints at it. "It's four past the hour of nine."

But this only produces a perplexed stare. "*Bitte?*"

"I say it's—bah!" And the old gentleman holds up the watch for his inquisitor to view.

"Ah! *Danke schön, mein Herr! Auf wiedersehen!*" With a polite tip of his hat, the little dandy strolls away, leaving the Captain muttering "Duced foreigners!"

****

Then it was finally time for me to craft a masterwork of impersonation.

IV.
The Belle of the Ball

Justice Blanford's parties are always social "events" and always attended by the crème de la crème of New Haven society. That Captain Wickman should be invited is clear cachet of his standing. He arrives just fashionably late, a little after eight of the clock, and is observed strolling casually up the marble front steps to the Honorable Justice's mansion.

Once his cape is secured with the servants, he takes a slow perambulation in search of his host through the chatting, laughing throng already in attendance. Apparently catching sight of the Justice across the room, the Captain makes in that direction.

When Wickman is a few paces away, his host likewise notices his approach. "Ah, Silas! There you are at last."

"Good evening, Charles. I want to say how pleased I was to receive your invitation."

"Nonsense. It wouldn't be a proper party without my old college friend. Here, I've someone I want you to meet."

With that, the Justice motions to a beautiful young woman who is standing to one side, sharing a feminine giggle with the Justice's wife. With a rustle of crinoline, the petite maiden—a feast for the eyes in a confection of pink silk well adorned with small bows and flounces—stands before the Captain.

"Silas, this is Miss Chastity Fox. You knew her late father, I believe. Old James Fox, the lawyer? Miss Fox, may I present Captain Silas Wickman."

The young woman curtseys and offers her hand to the Captain, which he makes a show of drawing to his lips. "Your servant, mistress."

With modestly downcast eyes she murmurs "And yours, sir."

Though she makes no overt show of it, she notices that the good Captain evidently finds it difficult to move his gaze away from the opulent show of womanhood that is the deep swoop of her décolletage.

His frown, and the hint of crimson high on his bearded cheeks, proclaim, at least to her, his opinion. *The fashion of this younger generation! Why, when I was her age, a woman would be ill-thought of indeed, had she appeared in public exposing so much of her—her—*

The Justice claps his old friend on the shoulder. "Miss Fox is here at my invitation tonight. She's without escort. Why don't you look after her? There's a good fellow."

The Captain starts to stammer a demurral, but the Justice is already moving off through the crowd.

There ensues an uncomfortable pause as the Captain scans the crowd, perhaps looking for a familiar face to include in this awkwardly intimate situation. The young woman simply stands there, a fetchingly innocent smile upon her full, rosy lips, her Irish lace-gloved hands modestly folded upon the shimmering volume of her gown.

She knows she is too lovely to be ignored for long. A shining cascade of russet tresses frame a heart-shaped face that is balanced on the threshold between childhood innocence and womanly beauty. Her skirts gently rustle and sway with each small movement as she stands patiently, demurely, her bodice catching the shifting glances of the golden illumination from the gas sconces, the frills and flounces that enfold her bosom—

Clearly frustrated in his search for someone to include in this conversation, the Captain clears his throat. "So. Old Fox's girl, are you? Knew your father in college."

She nods, and offers him a shy smile. "So I am told. And you knew the Justice too?"

"Indeed. Indeed."

The conversation languishes for a moment, then with a sudden spark of interest, she inquires, "Tell me, His Honor called you 'Captain.' Do you command a ship? I think that to be ever so romantic, to sail upon the vast ocean, visiting exotic lands, meeting Turks and Chinamen and wild heathens!"

The Captain replies with a gruff chuckle. "No, no. Haven't mastered a vessel in—what?— these eleven years. Sailing is a young man's game."

She raises her eyes to his, in sudden, touching earnest. "Oh, you must not say that! You do yourself insult to think yourself 'old.' There is ever so much difference between 'old' and handsome maturity such as yours."

Do her rosy cheeks take more color as she quickly drops her gaze to the hands that pluck in flustered embarrassment at a fold of her skirt?

To the Captain's obvious relief, a young cavalier at that moment presents himself and bows to the young lady. "Would you favor me with a dance, Miss Fox? The orchestra is about to play a reel."

But Wickman's relief quickly fades as his youthful companion turns up her nose, and makes a show of twirling her fan in her left hand. "Your pardon, sir, but the Captain has the first line of my card."

Rejected, the young beau trudges away. Her tone is cross as she watches him depart. "Oh, how I *hate* these parties. All those—those *boys!* Constantly hounding and pestering."

"He seemed a likable fellow to me."

That produces a petulant stamp of her dainty foot, which sets her full skirts swaying. "But they're such *children!* Their heads are always full of trivial toys like horses and sports. And how they prattle! Oh, I never should have come! I just know I shall be all evening with their silly chatter in my ears!"

Again turning those mesmerizing eyes full upon him, this time shimmering with open appeal, she lays a delicate hand upon his arm and pleads, "Please, won't you sign my dance card? Then I might at least have some refuge from their incessant demand!"

Since it would probably be impolitic to point out that those "children" are of an age with her, and at an apparent loss for how to otherwise politely refuse the entreaty of a damsel in such apparent distress, the Captain pulls a pencil stub from his vest and makes a notation upon the small embossed card dangling from her right wrist by a slender silken cord.

His reward is a radiant smile. "My savior!"

Again there is an awkward pause. As the young suitor had correctly claimed, the small orchestra has indeed struck up a lively air. A large space has been cleared at the center of the room, and there are already a dozen couples stepping lively to the tune.

For a moment, the enchanting feminine creature at his side gently sways to the tempo of the music, the lights shifting and shimmering upon her silken gown. It is more than the Captain can do not to gape at this enticing display.

Then, before he can avert his gaze and spare himself the guilty flush that accompanies being caught in a stare, she has turned to him and opened her arms in an obvious invitation. "Please, sir, dance with me! The music is heady and I want to join the fun!"

"Nonsense! Why I'm long past such foolishness."

With a winsome pout she points and says, "But look. The Justice dances with his wife and you and he are of an age." Then her expression becomes a playfully calculating smile. "Besides, have you not signed my card for the first dance? Are you so ungallant as to steal a woman's promise by such a deceitful trick, if you didn't mean to honor your pledge?"

He is still casting about for some excuse by the time she has taken his hand in hers and led him to the periphery of the swirling dancers. He *harrumph*s and grumbles—until she guides that same hand to the soft, smooth silk of her slender waist. Then they are spinning through the crowd, with sparkling laughter on her lips, and an unaccustomed smile blossoming upon his.

The smile mellows, perhaps with a small pang of remorse for the end of the tune and the polite applause of the dancers?

But when the orchestra begins another reel, and his young companion again opens her arms in invitation, his upraised hand and his gasped, "Got to catch my breath!" serves as adequate excuse. Instead of pressing her plea, she folds her arm in his and walks with him beyond the circle of the dance.

With his unoccupied hand he fans his flushed face. "Been too long. Out of fettle for such play!"

Her reply is more sparkling laughter and a tug toward the French doors that lead to the garden. "Come, a breath of night air will revive you."

Soon he finds himself in the moonlight garden, away from the bustle of the party. The scent of lilac floats on the warm evening air. She seems to glow with an inner light as she floats like a dream among the slumbering flowers. The silken murmur of her petticoats is the perfect counterpoint to the soothing hum of the crickets.

Suddenly she points. "Oh, see? A firefly! Isn't that magical?"

"Enchanting," he says, though the distracted tone of his voice suggests the firefly is far from his thoughts.

Catching that tone, she turns to him, her hands again virtuously folded upon her skirts. With eyes shining through lowered lashes she whispers, "It is a night for enchantment."

"This is wrong. I'm old enough to be your father."

The gentle, yielding pressure of her skirts against his legs as she leans upon his chest silences the voice. The soft caress of her silken glove upon his cheek stills any further attempt at objection. It takes little urging or guidance for his hand to seek the curve of her slender form. Her voice, as he finds himself again falling into the deep limpid pools of her eyes, is an intimate caress of its own.

"What do we care of that?" she murmurs. "Did I not say, 'a mature man'?"

Her parted, cherry lips demand his touch. She stands tiptoe as he bends forward to taste their sweetness.

The baritone voice is a sudden, shocking intrusion.

"Ah, Silas. There you are. I—what the devil?"

Suddenly the hands that had gently stroked his face are pressing against his chest with all her slender strength. The angelic purr of her voice becomes an anguished, frightened cry. "You beast! Unhand me! Justice Blanford—help! He's—he's trying to—"

"Wickman! Unhand her this instant!"

She succeeds in freeing herself from his embrace—the embrace that she initiated! With a swirl of skirts raised just sufficiently to reveal a parting glimpse of the delicate white lace of her under-dress, she flees back within the house, leaving Wickman to confront his glowering host.

He stammers, "Charles—it's not what it appears. She—she was the instigator. I—"

"Captain Wickman, how dare you! My own guest in my own house! I think it best that you leave. Immediately, sir—immediately!"

"But Charles!"

"Be gone this instant!"

The rest of the whole tawdry scene is a confusing blur as he recovers his cape and makes his chagrined escape.

V.
A Plot Revealed

The following morning, it was all I could do to delay my arrival at Niles's office until the appointed hour. The week for my "demonstration" had expired, and I had received word that I was expected at eleven of the clock, for another meeting with my two prospective associates.

I managed to restrain my enthusiasm, and appeared only three minutes early for the rendezvous. The same secretary again ushered me to the office's door, the carpetbag that was necessary for my proof being clutched in my right hand.

An anxious Niles and a very distracted Wickman greeted my arrival. As Niles was again rising from his chair to take my handshake, the Captain looked me once up and down, glowered at me and grumbled, "So? This is the proof? Looks the same to me today as he did on Monday!"

Ignoring Niles' outstretched hand, I calmly approached the Captain's desk, set my carpetbag atop it, and withdrew the first item.

A gnarled, well-worn hickory cane.

A quavering old woman's voice accompanied my gesture of discovery. "Is it proof ye're wantin'? Why then, 'tis proof that I have!"

A business card and a silver dollar.

Along with the uncertain, hesitant tone of a young boy: "I truly do thank you, sir—You shew'ed yerself to be a good man, an' I hope you think I'm right fer the job yo're offerin'."

A small, simple pocketwatch.

"Undt a vish der vatch I now giff, should you use. Der vatch in der pocket of der vest be'ink fast of two minutes."

And finally, a small, embossed card that was attached to a slender silken cord, displaying one penciled name upon its first line.

Accompanied only by a maidenly giggle.

The silence stretched for a full minute before the stunned Captain managed to finally gasp—

"By Jove!"

****

It took several minutes for the good Captain to recover his wits sufficiently that the conversation might resume. I think the turning point came for him when he had the happy thought that his reputation might no longer be in jeopardy.

In repayment for the night of discomfort I'd just put him through, I readily confessed Justice Blanford's co-conspiracy with me, thus confirming that the Captain's good repute was quite secure.

The Justice had given me a sealed note in exchange for my solemn promise to deliver the same, and this I now did. The Captain unsealed and read the note, his eyebrow rising, his expression becoming one of mortified amusement. His only comment as he tucked the note into his vest pocket was a grumbled, "Well, my friend, we'll take some thought for repayment, be sure of that!"

I'm amused to report that several times throughout the following hours, I caught the Captain appraising me with a calculating grin upon his face. (The report of how the Justice's perfidy was repaid, and my significant role in that enterprise, must wait for another day. It's quite the tale in its own right.)

Having finally laid the Captain's concerns to rest, we turned our attention to the business at hand.

I started the discussion by asking, "Well, may I take it as settled that my talents are suitable for the task you propose?"

To this both Niles and the Captain nodded agreement.

"Good. Having established that, might we now not turn to just what that project might be? What mission is it you wish me to undertake? What goal am I to pursue, and what shall be the means of accomplishing it?"

That produced a glance between my two associates. It was Niles who voiced their thought: "Nathan, perhaps you misunderstand. By your question, it seems that you think we propose a single, discreet action. Some singular endeavor."

I was perplexed. "Is that not the case?"

The Captain responded. "No. Think for a moment, boy. Going to spend a great deal of trouble and effort just to get you set up properly. Don't want to waste that on one little 'lark' when we might keep you about, sly and secret and ready to do all kinds of mischief."

This was not what I had anticipated. "What's to be the duration of this campaign?"

Niles shrugged. "Why, as long as possible, of course."

"What am I to make of that? 'As long as possible'? What 'possibility' might determine the duration?"

Another uneasy glance between my two companions provided the answer. Given the revelation I'd just attained, my words sounded surprisingly calm within my own ears. "Ah. The same 'possibility' that determines the career of any spy. The fact that once they're caught—they're hung, aren't they?"

To which, I received two nods.

****

The gist of what was envisioned by those two, unfolded over the next hour.

My thespian background had perhaps misinformed me somewhat as to the true nature of espionage and clandestine occupation. I had entertained the idea that my endeavors would find me alternately playing the coquette or the unsuspected old woman by day, conducting reconnoiters safely shielded from suspicion, my true nature and intent concealed beneath the innocent-seeming façade of a woman's garb and character. Only to subsequently shed my lace and satin for the dark-embracing cloak of the man of action, as I carried out nefarious and daring deeds under the cover of night.

I was quickly disabused of this notion.

"No, no, Nathan," said Niles. "You misunderstand completely. Tossing bombs and the dagger in the night is all very well, and probably helpful in some regards, but there is a much greater prize to be had simply for the taking. If the operative is clever enough, that is."

I was perplexed. "What prize might that be?"

Wickman's gruff voice supplied the answer: "Information."

Niles nodded. "Think for a moment. What good are all the arms and all the finest men if the enemy's location is unknown? What if, while we fortify some locale in unassailable strength, the enemy is busily circumventing all our preparation to strike in some unlooked-for place? Contrarily: What if we know in advance of the enemy's preparation, so that we may be the ones to circumvent and evade *him*?"

I looked from face to face. I admit, the prospect of this undertaking was suddenly looking the more attractive in my eyes. My stature, my upbringing, none of this suited me for the role of dashing bravado. I would have undertaken that adventure, to this day I truly don't know why. But to find that what was required was not physical prowess but rather subtle intrigue—wits rather than brawn—here was something I felt well within my scope, a field of endeavor wherein my talents might well be considered, with all humility, to exceed that of the commonality.

So I smiled as I asked, "So then, that is to be the task? The simple gathering of intelligence?"

Wickman "harrumphed" in a fashion I was quickly coming to inextricably tie with the old gentleman. "You needn't grin so easily, nor say 'simple' so quickly. Don't for a moment think that there aren't those on the other side just as clever, and just as slick with a bit of deception, as you. And don't suppose the information that we'd find valuable is simply lying around for the easy taking. That's the funny thing about secrets. Folks that have them, like to keep them. Don't like to share them, you know."

Niles hurriedly interjected, "Oh, to be sure, there will be times when it will be as simple as viewing some emplacement, identifying the division of troops engaged in its defense, the quality of the fortifications—things easily and innocently observed by someone with your knack for appearing 'harmless', shall we say?"

Wickman drove on relentlessly. "But more often, the intelligence we want will be hidden. Guarded. And by vigilant, intelligent folks. The minute you start thinking it all an easy lark is the minute that somebody will be measuring your neck for a rope."

Poor Niles, the "salesman" of this project, glared once again at his superior and visibly curbed some retort. He needn't have bothered. In fact, I found the Captain's candor encouraging, both for his honesty with me and for the implied competence of my new associates.

If they told me to consider the strengths of our enemies, of their capabilities, then my compatriots were approaching this whole affair with due caution and sobriety. And that could only work to my benefit.

"Gentlemen, suffice it to say, though I may not yet understand all the particulars of this line of work, you may take it that I am more than sufficiently convinced of the gravity and, let us be frank one with another, the danger inherent. Yet I vow that I'm still willing to undertake the task. Perhaps more so now than before. Now that I begin to grasp something of what is expected of me."

We all spent a moment gravely examining each other. It seemed that in that moment some unspoken pledge was taken, each from the other, and a compact was sealed. We three were now a team. It was a strangely solemn moment that I still clearly remember all these years later.

****

The moment passed and Niles rubbed his hands together. "Well, shall we not now take some thought as to the first move in this chess game we're proposing?"

I leaned a bit forward in my chair. "Indeed. I'm most curious to know the specifics of our match with our Southern neighbors. And so, at last, do we not come to it? Shall I not now, at last, be informed of the nature of my first undertaking? And before you answer, might I not now offer the guess that, throughout, you have had in mind for me some initial impersonation to undertake? Some persona that is to be my entrée into our foe's domain? Surely, that is not too far-fetched a supposition?"

Niles and The Captain exchanged a glance; and then it was Niles who, with a grin, replied, "Indeed, your conjecture is correct. We do indeed have your first characterization selected."

"As I thought." I waited with an expectant lift to my eyebrow, but nothing further was forthcoming.

I prodded again. "Well? Surely I am to be informed of the nature of this characterization at some point, am I not?"

Still Niles grinned. "Indeed you are, Nathan. And to acquaint you to your soon-to-be identity, there's someone I want you to meet."

VI.
Hattie

I first met Hattie the morning after my second audience with Niles and Wickman—that meeting whereat the former had suggested that someone else must begin to answer my question regarding the characterization I was to undertake. We had parted with the understanding that this mysterious individual would call upon me at my residence the following morning.

And so she did.

How shall I begin to describe Hattie—that most remarkable of women—that the reader might begin to understand the nature and character of she who was to so closely share all the coming trials and hardships with me?

I could begin by saying that when I answered the knock upon my door—a knock that came at what for a person of my nocturnal habit was an unseasonably early hour of nine of the clock—that I opened the door of my lodging only to encounter a well-dressed and seemingly genteel Negress waiting upon my welcome.

She was of slender, though most feminine form. Her features were delicate, calling to mind perhaps some princess of ancient Ethiope or mysterious Aegypt. The tight ebony curls beneath her fashionable bonnet were close-cropped, standing out from her head by no more than an inch or two. Her eyes were large, dark, almond-shaped and cat-mysterious. A pert, up-turned nose, high, aristocratic cheeks and full, generous lips completed her lovely countenance.

As I say, she was most fashionably dressed in a russet-colored dress with full hoop skirt. The hand that passed me her card was encased in an expensive-looking crocheted glove. She said, "Your pardon, sir. Have I the honor to address Mr. Nathan VanHorn?"

I drew the lapels of my dressing gown a bit tighter over my indifferently-buttoned shirt and nodded. "The honor is mine, I'm sure, Miss—"

Here I finally stole a glance at her card. "Miss H. M. Hamundsen," and an address not far from my own residence.

"—Miss Hamundsen. Um, to what do I owe the honor of this visit?"

She regarded my perplexity with an impish smile dancing upon her lips. "If I were to say that we share mutual acquaintance with Messieurs Wickman and Niles, might that not be sufficient cachet to allow me entrance, the better to confer the more discretely?"

Finally remembering my manners, I quickly bowed this exotic lady into my sitting room.

I'm sure I appeared to her as an unmade bed with legs.

Here I must digress for a moment and once more tire the reader with my upbringing and character, in that they bear so closely upon my initial relationship with Hattie.

My family was genteel, as I have already said. We moved within that circle of society that nowadays is vulgarly called "upper middle class." Our acquaintance, our association, the haunts we frequented—

How shall I say it without further adding to the low opinion that the reader has surely already formed of me?

I deny bigotry. My sin was ignorance, not intentional bias.

On that first day, seated there in my lodgings with this woman who so soon would become one of the people ever highest in my regard—I confess I saw only a dusky-hued Negress deporting herself, and dressing, above the norm for her race.

Dearest Hattie, with her keen perception and sagacious knowledge of human nature, I wonder: Did she see my disdain upon our first meeting? The disdain whose memory, to this day, still brings a flush of embarrassment to my cheeks? If she did, was it the mark of her superlative character that, seeing it, still she trusted me—accepted me?

So we sat there, in my rooms. She primly perched on my settee, I fidgeting in my wingback chair. An instant's silence was too uncomfortable so, perhaps too quickly and forcefully, I began: "Well, then. You are an employee of the Captain's, are you? What is your function within his organization?"

She folded her hands in her lap and murmured, "Why, it is to be much the same as your own occupation, or so I am given to believe."

The embarrassing incredulity showed clear in my words. "*You?* You are to be a spy?"

She raised dark, frank eyes to my own. "That surprises you?" There was a moment's quiet consideration. When next she spoke her tone was neutral—noticeably so. "Do you think a *woman* incapable of such activity? Do you think a woman will be found lacking in the requisite wit or courage?"

The rest of her question, she left unspoken: *Or do you think me lacking the wits to spy because I am Negro?* That unspoken rebuke turned my face red.

In answer to her spoken questions, I said, "Why, not at all. I am quite satisfied that if the Captain, being the—shall we say, 'cautious'?—student of human qualification that he is, finds you apt, I shall have no cause whatsoever to complain."

She lowered her eyes and that impish smile returned to her lips. " 'Cautious.' That's an interesting euphemism for the good Captain's misanthropy."

I began to share her smile. "Not misanthropy, surely?"

Still smiling, she shook her head. "No. You're right, that is too hard. 'Cautious' will do."

I motioned to my small pantry. "I was just boiling water for coffee. Might I offer you a cup?"

She nodded. "That would be most kind."

With coffeepot in hand, I returned a moment later. When we were provided and I had again claimed my seat, the discussion resumed.

"Miss Hamundsen—"

She waved a dainty hand in dismissal. "Please, sir, if we are to be associates—close associates, as I am given to understand—I think you should call me 'Hattie'. At least in those cases when I am not engaged on some other personification."

I sat up a bit straighter in my chair. " 'Personification'? Am I to understand that you are an actress?"

She shook her head. "No, I am little more than what you see before you, with no claim to any especial talent in that regard. Certainly no such talent that I would boast against your own."

Ever the vainglorious actor, I asked, "You know of my work?"

She nodded again. "But of course. Who in New Haven could attend the theater regularly and not know of your fame?"

"*You* attend the theater?" Would that I could have slapped my hand over my mouth before that utterance with its hateful emphasis on the word *you*, and therefore the renewed implication against her people could have slipped out. To her credit, if she noticed the implied slight, she graciously overlooked it.

"At every opportunity. Just recently I enjoyed your portrayal of Cordelia in *King Lear*. I must say, the production was well staged and all the parts were well enacted. Well, with the unfortunate exception of the actress portraying Regan. I found her to be no more than shrill, and quite overblown."

I nodded. "Indeed. I too thought her choice for the character to be quite ill-considered. Especially when you remember that Arden Leigh, an actress perfectly suited to the role, was at the time of casting, available to—"

I broke off my inane chatter to realize that my guest was smiling quietly into her coffee cup. My earlier slight regarding the unlikelihood of her being capable of enjoying the theater had, of course, not gone unnoticed. Her insightful comment as to the quality of an actress's performance was gentle reproof of my boorish presumption. Still, to her credit, she made no further comment on the matter, instead sitting quietly sipping her coffee.

This I can say for myself. Of all the faults I've catalogued, and the many I have not, I can claim as a virtue the willingness to humbly admit mistake and to sincerely beg pardon and enlightenment.

"Hattie. If you can forgive ignorance, please forgive me. I can offer no other excuse."

For a moment longer she smiled, then she nodded. "Mr. VanHorn—"

Now it was my turn to wave her to silence. "No. If, as you say, we are to be associates, and if you are willing to honor me by accepting the offer, please call me Nathan."

Again the dark depth of her eyes met mine. "Nathan, I do not forgive when ignorance causes slight, for I do not consider unintended harm to be cause for forgiveness. Only sadness. In my life I have learned that there is more than enough intentional hurt and harm to demand all of the forgiveness of which a person is capable. No, only when ignorance is willful, do I take offense."

I gazed into this remarkable woman's eyes a moment longer, then quietly I said, "Hattie, as I would not be the cause of sadness, would you consider to undertake my education? I'm quick enough a study that, with guidance, I can promise I won't often tread on toes I've previously bruised."

Again she favored me with a strangely haunting smile. "Then you should be a most welcome dancing partner, Mr. VanHorn, and I'd be glad of your company."

After a shared moment of polite smiles, I set my coffee cup aside and, in more sober tones asked, "But now, to business, if we might?" She nodded, and I proceeded: "It was my understanding that you were to give me some inkling as to the nature of the characterization I was to undertake for our 'employers.' Is this in fact the case?"

Matching my shift to the more purposeful mode, Hattie too set her cup aside, again folded her hands in upon the curve of her skirts, and nodded. "That is so. Hmm, how to begin? For it is a long and rather complex tale."

"Perhaps it would be best to begin at the beginning?"

Hattie's charmingly subdued smile again graced her lips. "Indeed. That seems always prudent. Very well. Let me tell you a story, Nathan.

"Some fourteen years ago, on a plantation not far removed from the city of Charleston, South Carolina, there lived a family named Bonveneau. This family was moderately well-to-do. Their ownership of a medium-sized acreage permitted them to retain the services of a corps of some twenty or so slaves, who toiled in their fields and served their domestic needs. At the time of my story, the family Bonveneau was a very small one, consisting solely of the father and his then five-year-old daughter named Katherine. This poor child was recently bereaved of mother, she having died in an accident two years previously. It therefore fell upon Katherine's nurse, or 'mammy' as such Negro servants are styled in the South, to supply such maternal tenderness and nurturing as the child might expect."

I nodded my understanding of this fairly prosaic state of affairs, which even I, mostly ignorant of the customs of the Southern gentry, was aware of.

Hattie continued: "But cruel Fate had more disappointments in store for this unfortunate child. You see, her mammy, whose name was Maddie by the way, was an unhappy woman herself. Her husband had been sold to a distant plantation some years previously. Since that time, Maddie had chafed against the bonds of slavery that bound her—that denied to her the love of husband that had been, but for one other, the sole joy in her life. Finally, able to bear the sorrow no longer, Maddie determined to escape to the North and freedom. It was her intent to make there such life for herself as she might; and then, through some as yet unknown method, promote the escape of her beloved husband and his own flight to freedom."

Would that I could say that such tragic tales as this were uncommon at that time. Such was hardly the case, however. Being closely acquainted with the theater of the day, I had heard variations of this sad history, often told as a fertile basis upon which to base many a heart-rending melodrama.

Hattie spoke on: "But Maddie's plan was never to be fulfilled. During the perilous flight to the North, she contracted a fever that ultimately claimed her life. She died after only three short days in a 'Free State,' living in such freedom as was to be had in a mean tenement."

There was a long moment's pause, which I was loath to interrupt. Finally, in the interest of the greater scheme upon which we were embarked, I gently asked, "But how does all this relate to you or to the matter—"

Then, before Hattie could answer, I suddenly understood. "Oh. As you said, Maddie's lost husband was her sole joy *but one*. Maddie had a daughter, did she not? A daughter named Hattie?"

A nod.

"A daughter who fled with her mother to the North, and upon her mother's death, became a foundling in a foreign land?"

Another nod and a soft voice that resumed the tale. "I was taken in by a Quaker preacher who resided in a little town in central Pennsylvania. Perhaps you know of it? Lebanon?"

But I could only shake my head in ignorance.

"Ah, well. In any event, he was a good and kind man. A widower, then several years bereaved, he raised me as well as any child could have hoped, with ample respect and love. Not only that, he was a very learned, well-read man who took great pains for my enlightenment. It was he who finally found the means and opportunity to nurture the spark of inquisitiveness I've always possessed. He was the Reverend Edmund Hamundsen, and his memory is as dear to me as any I hold. Upon his death two years ago, and supplied with such small inheritance as was his worldly wealth, I moved about for a time, finally settling in New Haven."

There was another moment's quiet introspection, as Hattie's mind wandered over memories of a life so alien to someone of my privileged station and upbringing that I could but sit in silent wonder at the nature of the person formed by these travails.

Yet, at length, a nagging question forced itself from my lips: "But this still leaves unanswered what the whole has to do with my entrée into the South. How does this epic— and please believe that I mean no disrespect to you or to your tale—how does this bear upon whatever personation I am to undertake?"

Hattie lifted dark, thoughtful eyes and regarded me with speculation. "Why, Nathan, shouldn't it be obvious by now? If you are to impersonate Katherine Bonveneau with some facility, surely it would be advantageous to have at your side a person intimately acquainted with that young woman's history, would it not?"

****

The next morning found me once again attendant upon my superiors, Niles and Wickman.

"Well, gentlemen, I am now a good deal more informed as to what is proposed, but there are several remaining details which I should like resolved."

The Captain turned in his chair, his attention apparently wandering as Niles dipped his head in a small nod and replied, "Of course, Nathan. What do you wish to know?"

"Well, my first question is: How am I to replace the person of Katherine Bonveneau? By that I mean, how is she to be removed so that I may take her place?"

"Ah, well. That brings us to the heart of our proposed scheme. To understand that, you must understand a little of what it is that the good Captain and I do. You see, it has been our function to comb the general populace with an eye toward persons of special ability whom we might engage to assist in our various projects."

"Of course. That was how I came to your attention."

"Just so. It was also how Miss Hamundsen came under our eye. We have been paying particular attention to expatriate Southerners and to absconded former slaves. In Miss Hamundsen, we found a very apt mind and a willingness to serve our cause. But, at the time, we could see no fruitful way to make use of her willingness."

The Captain, still staring off into space, grumbled, "Tell him about the newspaper article."

Niles glanced aside, with an expression of pique appearing and then quickly vanishing from his face. "Uh, yes. I was just coming to that."

Turning back to me, Niles continued, "It was just last week that Miss Hamundsen brought to our attention a small notice appearing in the *London Times*, for a day some two weeks then past, the announcement of the betrothal of one Katherine Bonveneau to the son of some minor English nobility. Research proved that this was, indeed, that very same Katherine Bonveneau who had Hattie's mother as nurse."

I began to see how the scheme was to unfold. "Ah! So, with her marriage, Miss Bonveneau will be removed from the playing field."

Niles nodded.

But almost immediately I shook my head. "But that won't do. Surely this whole situation won't create a vacancy into which I may step. Katherine is leaving her home, not staying. Her father will surely—"

Niles had raised his hand to interrupt my thought. "No, no, Nathan. You do not yet comprehend the entirety of the situation. You see, it has been many years since Katherine resided in her native circumstance. Upon the death of her mother and the subsequent absconding of her nurse, Katherine was sent abroad to an English finishing school. There she has resided for some thirteen years. So, it is not a case of her leaving her home in the South. Further, as to her father, well, there is where random chance has operated to furnish the pivotal point around which this whole plot revolves. You see, sorrows seem to dog Miss Bonveneau. Almost upon the heels of her announced betrothal came news of her father's demise."

"He's dead?"

The Captain replied, "As dead as Julius Caesar. Thrown from his horse, cracked open his skull. Now do you begin to grasp the scheme?"

"Indeed I do. So, it will be simply a matter of appearing at Katherine's old home in her assumed guise—the long, intervening years and separation being sufficient to cloud recollection and thwart recognition."

Again Niles nodded. "Just so."

Then another objection occurred to me and I gave it voice. "But, see here, there is still a substantial hindrance, or I'm very much mistaken. Won't Miss Bonveneau's neighbors take it as very much amiss when, instead of assuming residence in England, she suddenly appears upon her doorstep, still quite unmarried?"

Niles shook his head. "No. We have it on the authority of our resident informant that the matter of Miss Bonveneau's betrothal has not come to the attention of her old community. Put the lack of note down to her long absence and the paucity of close kin to trumpet the news. Indeed, it seems at least probable that intelligence of the coming nuptials didn't reach Mr. Bonveneau in time, and even he wasn't aware of them prior to his death."

Endeavoring to appear polite, I clicked my tongue and sighed, "How sad."

And then I realized what had just been said, and leaned forward in my chair again. "Hold up! Did you not just say, 'our resident informant'? Do you have agents already in place within that community? If so, what the duce do you need me there to undertake? Why risk myself if—"

Niles was already waving his hands. "No, Digny is hardly what we'd consider an 'agent.' Oh, hardly that!"

From the smile on both Niles' and (surprisingly) the Captain's lips, I got the distinct impression that my suggestion was wildly inappropriate.

Again Niles explained: "Digny is an old friend of mine. We read for the Bar together, you see. In Philadelphia. Now, don't misunderstand, Digny is a wonderful fellow. Intelligent, to be sure. Very decent and faithful and, I've no doubt, a valuable asset to our work. But—oh, my—hardly of the cloth to be an espionage agent."

The Captain summed it up in his usual epigrammatic fashion: "Fellow's a twit."

I tried to suppress a grin.

Niles' mouth quirked in a little moue of pique, but his tone was level enough. "Hmm—yes."

He addressed all of the following to me: "You see, Nathan. Digny is a Southerner, born and bred in Charleston. He supplies us with such information as comes his way, such information as he thinks we might profitably use."

The next was delivered in an acerbic tone—meant, I'm sure, more for the Captain's enlightenment than mine. "His pro-Abolitionist sentiments are well known to his neighbors, so you can understand that his efforts on our behalf are limited at best, his activities being subject to no little scrutiny by the Southern authorities."

Then in a normal voice, Niles resumed: "But what he can provide, he does. In this particular matter, and better than we could have possibly hoped, it seems that in his profession as attorney, Digny has just been retained to handle the estate of—yes, I can see by your expression you have guessed it—one Edgar Bonveneau, Katherine's late father. In that regard, Digny has been in correspondence with Miss Bonveneau, the sole heir, for the management of her father's bequest: that same plantation named Belle Bois. Better still, Miss Bonveneau has instructed Digny, by properly attested documents, to liquidate the entirety of her father's estate, converting the profits to cash that he is to transfer to her in England."

I crossed my legs in thoughtful pose, my expression, I'm sure, rather smug. "But with this Digny as accomplice to keep the secret, there shall be no one the wiser when, instead of disposing of her bequest through sale, a counterfeit Katherine returns at last to reclaim her home. Thus establishing 'herself' in the midst of the enemy in a most prosaic and unsuspicious fashion."

Both gentlemen favored me with hopeful expressions. In eager tones, Niles replied, "Exactly! Well, then. Now you know the whole of the proposal. What do you say, Nathan? Will you undertake this?"

It was with my accustomed rascally grin that I replied, "For all the fortuitous happenstance that has coalesced to make it possible, how could I refuse? It would surely be tempting Fate *not* to undertake this proposal!"

Even the Captain's face bore a smile when he rumbled, "Excellent!"

VII.
Missy Kate

Two weeks later found me in the persona of Katherine Bonveneau, standing at the rail of the Confederate blockade-runner *Elsie Boone*, watching the sea birds wheel above the salt waves some dozen miles off the coast of central Georgia.

To characterize as 'adventurous' the subsequent days between then in Captain Wickman's office, where I had agreed to undertake this adventure, and now, would be as much understatement as to characterize a flame as 'hot'.

And almost as unpleasant, in the enduring, as holding one's hand in that flame.

With the plan agreed to, events were quickly set in motion. Before the end of the next week, a multitude of preparations had been completed. (Many of the details of which shall eventually become clear.) Eventually, Hattie and I found ourselves, and our necessary luggage, sneaked aboard a purportedly Dutch merchantman of somewhat— shall we say 'ambiguous'?—registry. Provided with a forged manifest and logs that indicated a departure from Liverpool, the vessel slipped its moorings and quietly crept out of New Haven in the impenetrable depths of a truly memorable Thursday night.

Several days later, although it was Nathan and Hattie who had taken great pains to embark in New Haven unobserved, it was "Katherine" and Hattie who made no secret of their arrival in Halifax, Nova Scotia, and then of their "transshipment" aboard a vessel by the name of *Elsie Boone*.

The *Boone* was a blockade-runner that irregularly plied the perilous route between Confederate-sympathetic Canada and the Union-guarded shores of Georgia.

I must here relate that while our confinement aboard the "Dutch" trader had been by far the least comfortable or commodious sea journey I had ever yet endured—not that up to that point in my life I was much traveled upon the ocean— compared to claustrophobic closeness of the *Boone*, the Dutchman was a veritable floating vastness. Given that the *Boone* was built for speed and maneuverability, what little surplus space was available had been almost completely dedicated to cargo. Hattie and I were thus reduced to sharing a single cabin—of the approximate dimensions of the larger of my walk-in closets back home. We nevertheless managed to quickly arrange our situation so that at least a minimum of privacy, and thus decorum, was possible.

Fortunately, on this journey the *Boone* entertained but one other passenger: a painfully awkward young fellow by the name of James Eddiborogh, who was traveling south on some ambiguous errand, at the behest of some undefined department of the Confederacy.

In any event, though the voyage was a sore test of patience and privacy, the days of our passage were finally accomplished until we at last bobbed on the ocean in international waters, our final destination a dark line on the distant horizon.

****

Now the sun was rushing toward that western horizon.

As soon as twilight was full upon us, *Boone*'s master, Captain Hogueland, had assured us we would attempt the gauntlet of Federal gunboats he suspected lay in wait for us at the mouth of Savannah's harbor.

A sudden, errant gust of wind threatened to lift my skirts, and I was constrained to remove one hand from the railing, the better to constrain my willful garments and thus defend my modesty. From the corner of my eye, I spied my companion at the railing, young Eddiborogh, stealing a covert glance in my direction.

Saucy rogue!

Well, why should he not enjoy the spectacle of prim, virginal little Katherine Bonveneau wrestling with her treacherous satins and crinolines, struggling to preserve the chastity and propriety she had maintained so staunchly for this two-week-long sea cruise down the Eastern Seaboard? He had, after all, been the perfect gentleman for all of our constrained closeness within the *Boone*'s 110 feet of length these past two weeks. I deemed his forbearance a sign of quality and the mark of a gentleman.

That I was not a gentleman, but rather the rapscallion I've always claimed to be, was proven by my continuing test of his good character.

Judging the next gust of wind to a nicety, I "carelessly" raised my hand from my dress and began to return it to the rail. Just in time for the next puff of breeze to lift my skirts fully above my knees—displaying for all of the world to see, my silken hose, ruffled white-satin pantalets, and generously embroidered petticoat.

Uttering a cry of dismay, and hoping that my immersion in my role was sufficient for there to appear a blush of maiden's modesty on my cheeks, I removed both hands from the railing, the better to chivvy my rebellious attire back into decorous order.

Better than I could have hoped, my good feminine ally, the *Elsie Boone*, choose that exact moment to pitch a bit more forcefully than usual into the trough of the next wave. Off balance, my hands still engaged in preserving propriety and therefore unavailable to grasp the rail, I teetered for an instant before I felt a strong touch upon my shoulders.

"Have a care, Miss Bonveneau, or you'll pitch over the rail sure!"

I allowed myself to lean into James' embrace for a moment. Just long enough I calculated for him to realize he'd laid hands upon me, before I pulled back with sufficient force to show him that his touch, though welcome enough to prevent me from coming to harm, was still not proper considering the difference in our (apparent) gender.

I had to stifle a grin when he withdrew his hands with such alacrity you'd have thought he'd laid them on a hot stove. He was a gentleman, of that there was no doubt. I resolved to refrain from any further test of his manners.

Besides, if we were to dock tonight, there would be scant opportunity.

"Oh, Mr. Eddiborogh! I—" I laid a fluttering hand against my bosom and tried not to swoon. A good performance all in all, if I do say so myself. "What would have become of me if you'd not been here? You are surely my savior, sir!"

He smiled and waved a deprecatory hand. "Why, none of it. I merely joked. There was no real danger, though I was only too happy to, um, to—"

Seeking to regain his stature in my eyes, he nodded his chin at the gently rolling waves. "Still, the sea can be a harsh, unforgiving mistress. My years upon it have surely taught me that, if nothing else."

Since I had good intelligence from Captain Hogueland that James' "life upon the sea" in fact consisted of but five years as a river/harbor pilot, his implied braggadocio failed to produce much of genuine admiration in my male opinion.

Not wishing to bother with the effort of feigning feminine interest, nor of giving James the conversational upper hand at this point, I didn't pursue his proffered gambit, saying nothing at all in reply.

Failing of his attempt, he lapsed into embarrassed silence, and I acceded to the demands of my role and turned an again (hopefully) blushing countenance to the one hand I had now laid firmly and fixedly against my traitorous skirts.

James flailed for some new conversational ploy to cover the awkward ensuing moment.

"So, um, I assume you'll be happy enough on the morrow to be on dry land again. To finally be off to your estate."

Still gazing down at my hand, I assayed what I intended to be a small, uncertain, and sadness-tinged smile. "Oh, yes. It will be good to see Belle Bois again after all these years away. I only wish Papa might be there—"

Now it was my turn to lapse into a meaningful silence. A silence I accented by gently biting a quivering lip.

Again I had the better of the feckless Mr. Eddiborogh, as he struggled for some new escape from this increasingly ungainly conversational situation he had thrust himself into. "Oh, uh, your father, yes. Again, I'm so dreadfully sorry about his loss. I mean, your loss. To be but nineteen years of age and robbed of all living kin—"

Oh, heavens! A gentleman James might be, but such a socially inept young gentleman! Well, I'd invented the present situation, and now there was nothing for it but to play the role.

With the one hand still firmly planted upon my skirt, I raised the other gloved hand to Katherine's lips and stifled a sob.

James fluttered about in abject embarrassment at his latest gaffe: "Oh dear, oh d___nation! Your pardon, Miss Bonveneau! Oh, please don't cry! I—If there's ever anything I can do for you—you know, to help with—with whatever, you've only to call on me."

He attempted both to pat my shoulder reassuringly, and at the same time not to lay an unwelcome touch upon me. The result was a pantomime wherein his hand never quite came to rest on my shoulder, but rather always stopped short a fraction of an inch before actual contact.

I finally decided to let the poor wretch escape his predicament. Laying the hand that I'd just used to stifle my contrived grief, upon his hand, I pressed them both downward to rest upon my shoulder. Simultaneously, I offered him a tentative, but hopefully reassuring, smile. "Oh, James, thank you. Your kindness has been such a comfort on this trip. Truly, in this you have indeed been my savior. I don't know what I'd have done if I'd been forced to make this journey with only my Hattie for company."

Poor decent fellow. He produced the most embarrassingly grateful smile for my words. "Oh, you may be sure, Miss Katherine, it's always been my pleasure to share your company. I'm only too glad that you found my company agreeable as well."

I batted large sky-blue eyes at the object of my latest "infatuation," to which he only smiled the more broadly.

This possibly too-intimate situation was interrupted (and right at the most propitious moment, as always) by Hattie's appearance.

"Ah, dere yo' is, Missy Kate! I's been lookin' fo' yo' high an' low. If'n we's to get all yo' finery packed up, oughtn't we ta be about it?"

Showing off for this handsome beau, I turned an imperious eye toward my personal "darkie" and deigned to acknowledge her suggestion.

Then once again turning that shy, maidenly smile on James, I said, "I probably should be tending to final preparations. I do hope we'll see each other once ashore."

His head bobbed vigorously. "Oh, yes! That would be most agreeable. Perhaps dinner?"

Trying to moderate my joy at the prospect of his continued company, I dipped my head in a fine little maiden's curtsey and turned to follow Hattie.

Once we were safely below decks, and the door to our shared cabin was firmly shut behind us, Hattie turned a wickedly grinning countenance upon me and chided, "Nathan, honestly! Hasn't that poor boy suffered through enough of your 'flirting practice'?"

I could only blush—a genuine blush this time—and return my associate's knowing grin. "Well, who's to say where an ally might be found, eh? By sowing a few seeds now, when we've the leisure to do it, might we not at some future time reap an unexpected windfall?"

I doubted it, though. Most likely, once we reached Savannah, I would never see or hear James again.

Hattie only clicked her tongue, and shook her head at me.

****

As it befell, the Federals were somewhat lax that evening, and the good ship *Elsie Boone* slipped through the blockade without hail or challenge. (I can't help but wonder whether I had the clandestine efforts of Captain Wickman to thank for our apparent good fortune.)

A little after eight p.m., we were securely moored at Savannah's wharf. The passengers—being James, Hattie, and myself—were quickly disembarked. Our luggage was hoisted upon strong black backs to be transported to the Cumberland Inn, where we were to spend the night. At the Cumberland Inn, in the morning we would procure travel, each to his or her own destination.

The Cumberland was a very gracious establishment, redolent with Southern charm and hospitality. Our host, the Honorable Mr. Pennifarr greeted us at the door to the old manse that served as his hostelry. "Ah, welcome! Welcome one and all!"

James did me the courtesy of introducing me to my host. I smiled and contrived to look excited and a bit nervous at all the strangeness (as befitting 'an innocent young girl, fresh from the cloister of a English finishing school'). Mr. Pennifarr took note of my apparent unease, and patted my hand held in his. "Never you mind all the bustle, my dear. You're most welcome here."

I could only smile and again attempt a blush. (Drat! Of all the miscellany in my actor's bag of tricks, you'd think that the ability to counterfeit a simple blush would be one talent that might be included. Genuine women managed the trick with such ease. It fairly gave me pause!)

Chivying the sweating stevedores along with perfunctory commands, and directions as to which rooms to bestow our luggage, our good innkeeper then turned to us his guests and offered a formal bow. He then motioned us to follow him within.

The first of so many reminders of our current locale came when Hattie made to follow along at my heels. Pennifarr stopped dead in his tracks, and glared at her. Then, realizing that I might be ignorant of the protocols that obtained, his manner returned to the obsequious when, in helpful tones, he turned to me and said, "As to your nigger, Miss Bonveneau, for your convenience we've slave quarters just out back, above the carriage house."

I raised an eyebrow and made to object. It was good fortune that Hattie was close enough behind me that her nudge in my side went unnoticed by the gentlemen.

The words of my objection quickly became an imperious command: "Did you hear that, Hattie?"

She quickly bobbed her head. "Sho' nuff, Missy Kate. Dat fine wit' me."

It produced a small twinge in my conscience to grumble, "And did I inquire if that arrangement met with your approval? Now scat!"

Hattie bobbed her head, murmured, "Yes'm," and then quickly made to obey.

As I daintily lifted my skirts to the absolute minimum required to negotiate the steps, I suddenly realized that I'd have need for her in the very near future.

Pausing, I called after the retreating Hattie, "Once you're settled, see that you're in my room in no more than ten minutes. I'll want to dress for supper."

Again she bobbed her head and murmured, "Yes'm, Missy Kate." I was heartened to note a twinkle in her eye, as she too must have realized that it would not play well for anyone but her to assist me in disrobing.

Mr. Pennifarr called from the front hall (where he had come to a halt with James,) "Why, Miss Bonveneau, you needn't trouble about that. We've got several house niggers just for the convenience of our guests."

My initial reply was too brusque by half. "No!" Immediately I lowered my gaze, and moderated my tone to one more befitting the callow lass I pretended to be. "No, please, sir. I—Forgive me, but I find it *unpleasant* to disrobe in front of strangers, even darkies. I—"

And then I simply stared at the ground, desperately trying to convey the illusion of almost panicky modesty and shyness.

Evidently I succeeded well, for Mr. Pennifarr's tone became most conciliatory. "Ah! Of course, if that's your wish, why then that is how it shall be!"

Satisfied that my whim had been catered to, we all trouped within, Hattie now standing as unnoticeable to us as the hitching post left there for the convenience of the horses.

Our host conducted us to the second floor of his establishment. I soon found myself settled in a small bedroom most charmingly appointed in antique furniture, some of the items dating back perhaps as far as the Revolutionary War.

As soon as the door closed behind me, thus freeing me from the need to maintain my masquerade, I gratefully flopped down into the wonderfully soothing embrace of the four-poster bed, oblivious to the brazenly immodest disarray of my skirts. For the first time in several weeks, I finally stole a moment's respite.

****

Hattie was prompt in her attendance upon my need to dress for dinner, there in Mr. Pennifarr's lodgings.

Once the door to my room was again safely closed behind us, her impersonation, like mine, was quickly disposed of in the interests of efficiency.

For the male reader, I might digress for a moment and relate some of the less intimate intricacies that a member of the gentler sex endures for the management of her apparel, so that my circumstance might be better related. Indeed, for the feminine reader too, I might take a moment to describe the supplementary convolutions incumbent upon me to so successfully assume the outward show of her gender.

I had arrived upon the enemy shore with two large steamer trunks, in those days a fairly common amount of baggage for a 'young woman' of my station. Initial inspection of these two items would reveal nothing amiss. Or so it was fervently hoped!

A cursory examination would reveal a goodly number of dresses—assorted millenary—shoes aplenty—all innocent-seeming and innocuous. If one was to delve a bit deeper however, one would also find secreted in various drawers (and under layers of the most intimate apparel, I might mention) various items of theatrical makeup and supply. Also, if someone were to take an especial interest in the lining of some of the fuller skirts, he would discover, cunningly folded and sewn within, several complete suits of male attire ranging from shabby work-a-day rags to the finest of gentleman's evening attire. There was even the uniform of a Confederate Captain of Cavalry, complete with knee-length cavalier boots.

(Once we had finally arrived at Belle Bois, one of Hattie's first occupations would be to remove this male attire from its place of concealment, and then to find suitable hiding place for it all.)

However, not all of my feminine vesture had been drafted as sites for concealment. I had sufficient store of "normal" dresses, such that during my journey to Charleston ,I would never have to chance walking about with greater than normal maidenly concern for the concealment of what was beneath the surface of my attire.

Indeed, there was little enough that a genuine woman would find extraordinary in any of my store of costume, if the unusual nature of their linings were first removed. My stock of undergarment was, on the whole, indistinguishable from any other like-situated young woman. Here, the interests of propriety and modesty must limit the catalogue of "Katherine's" more intimate apparel. I will simply say that it was both complete and unremarkable.

"Unremarkable" but for two notable exceptions, that is.

Both of these items, one or the other of which was, perforce, upon my person at all times, had been contrived for me by a dressmaker of perhaps the greatest genius it has ever been my good fortune in my thespian career to encounter.

Her name is Abigail Yates, should any of you ladies have occasion to seek the services of a dressmaker/milliner of the absolute first order in your travels through New Haven. At the time of this writing, she still plies her needle within her shop in the Oakmont Hill neighborhood, just a mile north of the site of the new Opera House.

As I say, I have never met an artisan of skill commensurate with Abigail's. Self-esteem demands that I take due credit for my ability to impersonate the feminine gender; modesty demands that I give Abigail due recognition for the many costumes that allowed my performances to be as wholly believable as they were.

As I have heretofore remarked, my form, though certainly not overly feminine, was, at the same time, still very much the masculine version of my mother's. My natural inclination might best be summed up with the term *slender*. With a sigh, I amend that to *noticeably slender*. For Abigail, this presented a wonderfully "empty canvas" upon which to operate.

I have numerous feminine acquaintances that, aware of my feminine impersonations, have evinced sincere jealousy for the ease with which my already narrow waist can be molded through the application of a corset into such curvature as to positively embody the current monde.

A womanly curve to my hips, on those occasions when such was necessitated by the costume I wore, was easily attained by the lengthening and fashioning of my corset so as to include such cotton batting as Abigail felt necessary to produce the illusion. (Though I might mention, the then-current fashion of full skirt and bustle proceeding immediately from slender waist usually obviated such need.)

And speaking of curvature and padding, here I might return to the two aforementioned "special" items to which I previously alluded.

I can, with decorum I think, mention that almost any feminine impersonation must include provision for a maiden's bust. Usually, in creating my costume, Abigail again resorted to the application of simple cotton batting in such form, and in such measure, as she deemed requisite. For theatrical garb, in that there was no need for it to appear as more than it was, to wit that of a fantastical costume, this was wholly adequate.

However, once my impersonations had to pass the scrutiny of persons viewing it in everyday circumstance, and with no hint given as to the artifice that created the show, a much greater degree of subtlety was required. It would be most embarrassing indeed, and very difficult to explain, if some woman was for some reason to inspect one of my dresses, then to encounter, tailored within, a large amount of cotton padding in such locale as to render its apparently flat-chested wearer more buxom! No, in as far as it was practical, all of my clothing had to be as conventional as possible.

I'm pleased to report that Abigail, in her usually brilliant fashion, rose to the occasion.

She created for me two items of undergarb that might be worn beneath all my other feminine accouter. Each was intended to provide such —shall I say here, *curvature*?—as to promote the impression of normal feminine anatomy. Each garment was in form rather like a somewhat more "high-rising" than normal corset, being worn over my ribcage and proceeding downward such that its lower hem would lie beneath the lower hem of such regular corset as I might wear. Though each item bore this similarity, there the likeness ended, for each had been designed with an eye toward the dress it was to be worn under, and the ultimate illusion it was intended to produce.

The first of the two "corselettes" was the one that saw, by far, the greater service. (I believe I shall continue to style them *corselettes*, for that term aptly describes them.) It was of lighter, less constricting construction. It produced an admirable, yet not overly remarkable, bust through the employment of simple cotton batting, adequately placed and adequately formed by Abigail's cunning hand.

The second corselette was intended to address the then-current fashion that exposed so much of a young woman's décolletage. It might be wondered how this conjuring trick was accomplished. (That "trick" which I have previously alluded to, both in the mention of my enactment of Mistress Snake during my first meeting with Niles, and subsequently during my dalliance with Captain Wickman upon the singular occasion of Justice Blanford's soiree.)

I have said, and I maintain, that my natural form is not, and never was, particularly feminine. (Nor, admittedly, overmuch masculine.) Contrary to what some pundits have subsequently claimed when addressing my exploits, I do not, and never did, possess—how shall I say this?—an inordinately "womanly" upper torso. Candor and faithfulness to this narrative do force me to admit however that there must have been something of my mother's heritage in that part of my physical form, for I did have—shall I say "a relative abundance of spare flesh"?—about my chest.

This circumstance served both Abigail and myself well when the more "daring" of styles was attempted. Prior to my embarkation upon my espionage career, it was always suitable for the creation of my maidenly display to employ a tightly wrapped band of muslin about my upper chest such that the excess of my flesh was, by redirection in natural course, forced into the enlargement of—well—again, let me be discrete and say that the resulting illusion, which the reader must by now comprehend, always worked to a fare-thee-well.

For the conduct of my intelligence career, Abigail had refined this method—the redirection of my natural features into a more contrived form—and had incorporated the fundamentals of this trick in the second of my aforementioned corselettes. This device, by far the less comfortable and more constraining of the two, operated upon much the same principle as the binding muslin band. In this case, however, the operation was more in the form of an ordinary corset. Drawstrings served to tighten the garment and thus compress my flesh. This surplus was then, by the shape and fashioning of said garment, redirected as was desirable for the conduct of the disguise.

The finishing touch was the addition of two cunningly placed pads composed of very limber India rubber. I leave it to the reader's imagination as to just how, and for what effect, these two pads were employed.

I must say, on the first day when this particular device was demonstrated in the discrete dressing areas of Abigail's shop, though long-ago inured to the believability of which I was capable in my characterizations, still I found myself quite taken aback by the utterly convincing nature of the illusion.

This was especially so once a rather scanty chemise had been added over the top of, and thus concealing, the corselette. Indeed, by the trick of this devious bit of clothing, enough of my apparent buxom bust was so readily displayed, it fairly appeared that even a fraction more revelation would quite exceed the bounds of all propriety.

Odder, and more disconcerting still that such was Abigail's artistry and skill with the materials used, that a casual touch of the hand to that "flesh" (in reality, those aforementioned India rubber pads) that was concealed beneath the front of the chemise engendered no doubt as to the "reality" of that part of my woman's form either.

(So much so that I confess, when I first tried that experiment myself, a flood of color appeared on my cheeks when my hand encountered what, most assuredly, felt to be a very intimate part of a maiden's person.)

I may, with absolute conviction, assert that when either of these two devices, particularly the latter, were employed to good effect, any observer of either sex would have been insightful far beyond the common ken to suspect the true nature of the outward show I presented to the world.

VIII.
Belle Bois

The remainder of our journey to our ultimate destination, tedious though it might have been, was nonetheless unremarkable. At the time of our passage, the route we traversed from Savannah to neighboring Charleston, was as yet mostly untouched by the war. There was little clue as to the hardship and travail that was soon to descend on this admittedly lovely and pastoral bit of God's creation.

Indeed, the only hint of the looming war was the abundance of uniforms and the hustle and bustle of a society now directed to the conduct of armed strife.

Still, there was a definite "mood" of wary unease. Fortunately, our supposition that my apparently petite and wholly innocent outward appearance would serve to deflect suspicion proved to be universally correct. Always were Hattie and I met with solicitous concern, in my case, and with complete indifference and disregard, in Hattie's case.

If anything, it seemed that once it was determined that Hattie harbored no overt intention to flee from her situation, she moved with even greater ease through society than did I. It seemed almost that she was consciously, studiously ignored by the white southern gentry we encountered. I filed this fact away for future reference.

Hattie, of course, played her role faultlessly, sometimes taking even me unawares to the point that I reacted as one of my apparent station would react to such a menial-seeming creature. Bless Hattie, on those occasions I was always returned to reality by the sly little smile, and the twinkle in her eye, which were visible only to me.

****

The morning that followed our arrival upon enemy shores found Hattie and myself embarking for the last leg of our journey, aboard the "Charleston and Great Southern Railroad." As has been my experience with this form of travel, the appellation selected by the owners of this rail conveyance somewhat exceeded the reality of the situation. I cannot, with due candor, characterize this particular enterprise as but "modest", their claim to "greatness" notwithstanding. The carriages were a bit threadbare, and many sections of the track proved to be—well, the progress of our journey is best described as "less than placid."

Upon boarding our train, I moved to ascend into the car third-most rearward from the locomotive. It was my desire to minimize the accumulation of soot and ash, as far as was possible, upon the light blue gingham dress I had chosen for that day's wear. At the same time I still wished to maintain proximity to Hattie, embarked as she was aboard the cars set apart for the use of Negro passengers. As it is in the North, Negro cars were situated closest to the heat, smoke, and clamor of the locomotive.

For reference, I might say that we embarked at the station serving the colorfully-named hamlet of Cossawhatchie, South Carolina—at that time, the southernmost terminus of the aforesaid "C. and G. S." rail system, and the one nearest our port of arrival in Savannah.

Happily, our chosen carrier did display at least minimum efficiency, for our scheduled departure at eleven o'clock a.m. was overshot by the admirable time of only fourteen minutes' delay. A good performance by any standard, in those days.

As I say, the progress of our journey was not the least harrowing of such expeditions I have undertaken. Still, I can relate that Hattie and I arrived at the station in Summerville, South Carolina (being the station actually nearest to Belle Bois and therefore our point of debarkation) none the worse for wear, a little after four in the evening. The station attendants, (I noted the curious fact that the laborers were a pair of somewhat unkempt but sturdy white fellows of late-middle age, rather than the already more accustomed black male toiler,) set about quickly unloading my two steamer trunks and setting them aside on the platform for subsequent transshipment to whatever transport arrived for my conveyance to my new residence.

Ultimately, the train again *chuff*ed out of the station, and the handful of passenger disembarking with us quickly disappeared to whatever destinations awaited them. That left us, Hattie and myself, standing uncertainly on the now-deserted platform, cast adrift strangers in a strange land, waiting for recognition and greeting from whatever person had been dispatched for our escort to the plantation.

So we waited. And waited. And waited the more.

When the clock above the ticket-seller's window finally proclaimed the hour to be six p.m., and it became apparent that the station manager was contemplating the cessation of the day's business, my unease was sufficient that I determined to find the cause of our apparent abandonment. The bored little man behind the ticket window could offer no good intelligence as to the remedy for our situation. Finally, he advised that I might best employ myself by seeking out someone at the Hotel Ashley, an inn that he could, without troubling himself unduly, indicate from his perch upon his stool there in his cubicle. It was his suggestion that I might find someone of the hotel staff who could be dispatched to ascertain the reason for my seeming desertion.

Try what tricks and conceits I might—the appeal to his compassion for a poor, castaway maiden; the bitten lip: the large, beseeching eyes; the wrung hands and tremulous voice—this clod refused any further aid.

I was finally reduced to trudging off to the aforesaid hotel myself, leaving Hattie in charge of our luggage, with instruction to await me if our now long-tardy escort did in fact finally arrive. All the while I was muttering to myself, in a most unladylike and out-of-character manner (once out of earshot, that is) concerning the apparently shocking lack of the supposed all-pervasive Southern gallantry I'd heard so much about.

Little did I realize the depths of my ignorance as to the true state of things! Little did I foresee the method and degree as to the education I was about to receive!

I'm pleased to relate that my welcome at the Ashley Inn was far better than that I had received at the railroad station. Some small rumor of my coming had, apparently, been making the rounds and I was warmly welcomed once my (assumed) identity was known. The manager quickly discovered the cause of the lack of a reception awaiting me. It was the misunderstanding that my arrival was to occur some three days' hence. He quickly dispatched one of the inn's "pickaninnies" to my new domicile, to make them aware of my advent and my need for conveyance. In the meantime, I was most courteously invited to retrieve my luggage, ordering the same to be brought here where I might rest myself from my journey and await my transport.

Thanking the inn's staff, I made my departure to retrace my steps. At the entrance, a tall, well-formed gentleman held the door for me. I was preoccupied to the point that I paid him scant attention, only bobbing my head in acknowledgement of his service in opening the portal.

It was only as I swept past him that I saw the left side of his face. I think I gave a little start at his disfigurement. There was a broad, and judging by the light pink cast of the flesh, a fairly new scar that proceeded from his hairline downwards, to disappear beneath a cast covering his eye. Thence, the line of insulted flesh continued full to the curve of his jaw. The scar—I admit that I remarked it so fixedly that I had scant attention of a sudden for the rest of this good gentleman's person—was not of such character as would be produced by a sword wound. That is to say, it was not of a singular, "clean" line. Rather, it was composed of several broken and misaligned segments, as though the injury that engendered it was more in the form of a rending, mangling outrage.

I am sure my shock and disquiet at his distortion was clear to read upon my face. Yet his smile remained both easy and friendly. He returned the inclination of my head and calmly waited for me to resume my progress, which I quickly undertook.

Throughout the short journey back from inn to railway station, my imagination was preoccupied trying to guess the nature of that poor unfortunate's injury. Needless to say, the odds were good indeed that he had acquired his hurt at some recent point in the war. By this time, there had already been several major engagements and not a few small set-tos.

I remember I was thinking to myself what a cruel and needlessly hurtful place the world could sometimes be, when I rounded the corner of the now-closed train station and beheld a most frightening and infuriating sight.

The two white roustabouts that I have previously alluded to, (the same duo who had unloaded my trunks,) had apparently accosted Hattie as she dutifully guarded those items. It was clear from their shockingly close intrusion upon her person, and the lewd expressions upon their coarse faces, what their intent was.

Indeed, one of them was actually taunting her with, "Well Lem, like I says: I doesn't much care fer nigger wenches. But for such a pretty little bit o' calico as this 'un, I'd be sore pressed not to make a 'ception."

For a breathless moment I was so flabbergasted at the spectacle of such an outrage occurring out in the plain sight of any passing person, at the absolute unmitigated gall of its perpetrators—that I was rendered quite speechless. But when the speaker raised an uncouth paw toward the region of Hattie's bosom, the spell shattered.

Lunging forward, I barked (quite out of character, and in a voice perilously close to the masculine,) "See here! What are you two ruffians about?"

Both heads swung in my direction. The speaker, the apparent leader of the pair, contemptuously spat a dark brown quid, almost at my feet, and growled, "And what business is it of your'n what we's up ta?"

Finally remembering my need to retain my character, but still much too agitated and angry to manage more than the timber of my voice, I stabbed a finger at Hattie and exclaimed, "You will unhand my companion immediately! Immediately, do you hear?"

For the first time the second lout spoke. His voice was oddly slurred and halting. "Be this'n yo' niggah?"

Remembering more of my current locale and (supposed) station therein, I moderated my tone further and replied. "Yes, she most certainly is. Now, leave off your pawing of her, and go about your business."

But the leader was now rounding on me. "Say, you ain't from roun' hereabouts, are yuh? I knows mos' o' the gentry hereabouts, an' you ain't one o' 'em."

I sensed danger, but couldn't quite define its cause. "What has that to do with anything? Now, I'll say again, leave off your mischief and be gone, or I'll surely summon the law!"

The second ruffian, the one of slurred speech mumbled, "Maybe we'd bes' do lik' she say an' mosey 'long, Tad."

The leader turned to his accomplice and growled, "No fancy b___h g'wine tell me what I may nor mayn't do wit' no niggah, hers or not! Fo' that matter"—and here he turned a pair of greedy, piggish black eyes on me—"maybe I doesn't has ta settle fo' no darkie wench atall. Maybe they's better pickin's ta be had."

His accomplice was becoming nervous, casting a worried eye about for witnesses to this dreadful scene. "Tad—nah—do'n' think o' *that*. Tha's not right."

I found myself trying to back away from the ominous approach of the lead scoundrel. "Yes! Listen to your friend! Lay one hand on me and I'll—"

But my threats were falling upon deaf ears. I had backed against a wall and had no further avenue of retreat. The cad was upon me, one callused hand upon the curvature of my forged bosom, the other menacingly pressed against my throat. Had I been a true woman, I'm sure I would have instinctively given vent to such a scream of outrage and fear that the whole hamlet would have been roused to my instant rescue. Had I been a true man, more seasoned in the masculine mode of fisticuffs and vibrant action, I would perhaps already be giving good account of myself at this scalawag's expense.

But I was neither. And being neither, I lacked idea as to my action, and therefore was helpless to prevent this monster's attempt to fulfill his horrific intent.

All would have probably proceeded to what for me was a doubly disastrous conclusion, until I saw, from the corner of my eye, some small motion that gave me notice of the arrival of a new person there upon the platform of the station.

Before I had true comprehension of the course of events, my attacker had been forcefully thrust aside by this new arrival.

The very same scarred man who had held the door for me at the inn.

My aggressor stumbled back a few paces, and glared at my savior. The scarred gentleman returned the scowl, and in a voice that was deep, masculine, and very dangerous for its quiet intensity, said, "So, Tad. Up to your old tricks with the women again? You know, this is a good example of what always has been your problem. You never have learned your limitations. By my reckoning, fully three-fourths of the black wenches in this town are too good for the likes of you. I think before you aspire to even greater heights of criminal inadequacy with white folk, it's high time someone taught you just what your place is."

Obviously somewhat unsure of what my savior had meant by much of that speech, but gathering enough of its sense to get the gist, the ruffian growled, "An' yew intends ta teach it ta me, does ya? A one-eyed cripple like you? Best you shank it, Major, before I puts the light out on yer other lamp."

But 'the Major' was unimpressed by the villain's bluster. With that same quiet-but-deadly tone, he murmured, "Be smarter than you appear, Tad. Take your own advice and 'shank it' while you may. Stay a moment longer, and I'll make it hard on you. That's my final word."

There next occurred such a sudden flurry of activity that the whole is still a muddle in my mind. My scattered impressions may be summarized thus:

With a bestial rumbling in his throat, Tad produced a knife from somewhere within the folds of his threadbare coat, and sprang at the Major. At the same time, Lem, the second ruffian, apparently having had quite his fill of the whole proceeding, turned on his heel and made to flee. He had not gone two steps when Hattie, an animal shriek of her own upon her lips, sprang upon his retreating back, her hands reaching around to claw at his face. Meanwhile, the Major, with admirable economy of motion, had raised his left arm to block Tad's thrust. I noted, for the first time, that the Major held a straight, black cane in a gloved left hand.

I was aghast when Tad's weapon sank, with an horrific dull *thud*, into the flesh of the good Major's arm, midway between wrist and elbow.

More astonishing still, the impaling blow seemed to produce no noticeable effect upon that stalwart! (It was more abhorrent than I can say, to relate how I noted, in that odd clarity that accompanies such frantic action, that Tad's blow had been of sufficient force for the tip of his heavy blade to pass quite through the Major's arm, and that it was now protruding out of the sleeve of his coat on the other side!)

With calm deliberation, the Major's reply to this assault was a well-aimed blow delivered to Tad's nose with a strong right hand, the force of which sent the cur sprawling. Maintaining that admirable calm, the Major then unlocked what I now perceived was the sword within the sword cane he held in his left hand. He drew the blade. Before Tad could even begin to crawl away, the Major had the tip of his gleaming weapon pressed against the swell of Tad's Adam's Apple.

The mettle of the Major's character shown most clearly in that when he next spoke, his voice continued in that same deep, controlled, and dangerously soft tone that it had always possessed. "Though I think it quite unlikely you'll be able, if you can think of one good reason for me to spare your worthless life, Tad, now would be the time to make me aware of it."

But Tad was unmanned quite. He could only blubber, "Oh, no—oh, Major—oh, don'—oh, please don'!"

His lip curling in most understandable disgust, the Major contented himself with but pricking the wretch's throat before withdrawing his blade. "I wouldn't befoul my good metal with your filthy blood. Now then, lie still while we wait for the constable, or I might just lose my restraint and that would be a pity. It's such a bother to have to clean a blade."

Throughout all of this, Hattie and Lem had been wrestling about. She still was upon his back, industriously clawing at his face and neck, he was staggering about in a wild career, trying to dislodge the hellion bestride him. With a sudden clatter, Lem encountered the apparently unexpected edge of the platform. Losing his balance, he tumbled off the elevated planking to land in a heap upon the tracks, with Hattie still ascendant upon his back.

The awkward force of his landing apparently rendered Lem quite insensible, for he lay still as Hattie continued to rend and tear and scream unintelligible epithet.

Observing this, the Major turned to me and, still pressing the point of his sword against Tad's throat, he inquired in a most prosaic and conversational tone, "Miss, might I trouble you to restrain your servant? I fear she's quite determined to visit very lasting harm on poor Lem. Though he's a scalawag, I assure you that but for this one's urgings"—and here the Major applied just sufficient pressure to again prick the tender flesh of Tad's throat, eliciting a terrified squeak from that vile wretch—"Lem is not such a bad sort, all things considered."

The amazed funk I'd fallen into finally dissipated enough for me to attempt Hattie's restraint.

I finally managed to drag her away from her victim's insensible form, and to calm her to the point that she was content to simply gasp for air and glower at both villains.

Having sufficiently recovered my own wits to again assay the person of gentle Katherine Bonveneau, I turned limpid eyes on the Major and murmured, "Sir, but for your gallant intervention—well, I simply cannot even contemplate what might have transpired here."

I was again rewarded with that urbane smile. "Why, none of it, mistress. For the good account you were giving of yourself, I might have better employed myself in a leisurely notification of the constabulary."

I was mystified by this reply. "What do you mean? Of what 'account' do you speak?"

He nodded to the still insensate Lem. "Why, your efficient handling of that cur, of course. I realize that while a young lady of your quality would rarely so demean herself, I'm sure no one will censure you when it is understood that such forceful action as precipitating Lem's fall from the platform through the expedient of tripping up his feet was taken out of direst necessity to preserve your virtue. I would take it as the greatest compliment if you would call upon me to answer any who would dare to suggest otherwise."

I could only reply, "Sir—well, I'm most confused. It was through my stalwart Hattie's good efforts that yonder cad was forced from the platform and subdued, none of mine."

Here, the Major's smile departed; and in that now-accustomed quiet, forceful voice he said, "No Madame. Forgive me but in that you're quite mistaken. While I have no doubt of your servant's bravery and devotion to her mistress—qualities that I admire in a person, their skin color notwithstanding—still it was not she who rose to your defense and defeated Lem. You see, it shall be my testimony that throughout, your Hattie's conduct was as befitting her station. Since it is a flogging offense for a slave to manhandle a white person, good cause or no, and since it is my belief that your Hattie is in no wise guilty of anything that would merit punishment of any kind, it therefore follows as a logical progression that if I did not dispatch Lem, (being then otherwise engaged with subduing Tad,) and your Hattie did not dispatch Lem (it being quite beyond her station to do so,)—why then, it must have been your laudable efforts in your own defense that produced his capture. Wouldn't you agree, Tad?"

Another prick of the Major's sword, and a dangerous light in his eyes, quickly elicited a panicky nod and a plaintive "Oh, yassuh! That be th' way I see'd it!"

The Major smiled and nodded. "Good for you, Tad. Perhaps you're not quite so ignorant as you appear. Wouldn't that be a pleasant surprise?"

Tad's reply was lost in the sudden flurry of the arrival of the Town Marshal and his deputies.

As the deputies made to restrain the two ruffians, the Marshal, a portly little fellow with a monk's tonsure hairdo, turned to the Major and inquired, "Now then, what's all the ta-do here?"

Finally realizing what my role would here require of me, with timorous voice I leveled an accusatory finger at the two now-cowering curs and whimpered, "They—*they laid hands on me!* I believe that, but for this good gentleman's heroic intervention, they would have—would have—"

Have I heretofore mentioned I possess quite the knack for feigning a woman's weeping? Given the current monde within the theater for the so-called "melodrama," and the frequency with which it demands the copious and believable outpouring of strong emotion that so often in women finds expression in such outlet, needless to say that the ability to believably portray a woman's sobs is a mandatory skill in any actress's repertoire. Mandatory as well for someone, like myself, who would regularly undertake a woman's roles.

And I do it so well.

Laying a comforting hand on my shoulder, the Major casually remarked, "It would seem that I have cause to levy complaint as well." Removing that steadying hand from my shoulder, the Major, with unbelievable aplomb, and after a bit of coaxing, calmly removed the dagger from his left arm, (which in all the commotion I had quite forgotten,) and held it aloft for the Marshal's inspection.

Now my shock and sudden agitation were quite real. "Oh, sir! Your poor arm!" Turning to the Marshal I commanded, "Go! Fetch a surgeon at once!"

But the Major only chuckled. "No, no—mistress, please— don't trouble yourself. I'm quite unharmed. You see, prior service to country has left me uniquely suited for such occupation as that in which I just engaged. I can honestly reassure you, it's hardly more than a slight inconvenience to be stabbed in a wooden arm."

****

I came to discover that the name of my gallant rescuer was Major Everett Vincennes, formerly of the Twenty-Third Infantry Regiment of the South Carolina Volunteers, and just now completing an extended convalescence. (The reason for the convalescence being, of course, obvious.)

This intelligence was gathered for me by that same manager of the Ashley Inn who had previously been the first to offer me welcome to my new home. It was to the Ashley that the good Major and I repaired after the whole disagreeable business with Tad and Lem was sorted out, and those two ne'er-do-wells were carted off by the Marshal with dark threats by the latter of "long overdue reckonings." (Once the two miscreants were hauled before the local magistrate, that is.)

In our conversation, the subject of the good Major's injury was not broached. It seemed hardly a polite topic for me to assay, and I left the matter alone. For his part, the Major continued in that same flawlessly polite and genteel manner he had shown me from the first instance of our meeting. (That is, when he most courteously held the door to assist the progress of the young damsel he thought he beheld. I must say that the Major's manners were impeccable to the point that I'm quite sure, had I been in my masculine guise at the time, still would he have held the portal for me, he having arrived at the door first.)

Here, at last, I had finally encountered the flower of Southern chivalry I had been expecting.

Everett attended my wait, there in the common room of the Ashley, for the conveyance from Belle Bois. Once he had been appraised of my assumed identity, there ensued a disconcerting "reunion," when it befell that Everett was, in fact, a childhood playmate of Katherine's. I think I might say that I rose well to what was to become the first of many such meetings. As had been hoped, the distance of years provided me with ample disguise. I needed only smile shyly at shared reminiscence of long-bygone days, and feign delight at being rejoined with an old playmate whose memories seemed as time-shrouded as my own.

I had no hint whatsoever that I gave Everett any cause to suspect that I was not the person I pretended to be, for throughout our conversation, his manner was that of seeming-genuine pleasure and friendship.

But while I cannot recall anything that I said, or failed to say, that might have aroused the Major's suspicions this day, this does not mean that I indeed escaped suspicion. Subsequent events would hint as much.

Discovering that Everett's property was the next one south of Belle Bois, we gave mutual assurance of many happy meetings and conversations to come.

For me to do less must surely rouse suspicion. It had been expected that I would encounter persons of Katherine's acquaintance. But to have the actual event occur so soon upon the heels of my arrival—I suppose I had hoped for an interval within which I might gather sufficient intelligence, the better to manage my portrayal. But, as she so often has in my life, Dame Fortune made her differing plans for me quickly known.

After the passage of an hour and odd minutes from the time of Tad's attack upon my person, a carriage and a wagon appeared in the lane outside the Ashley. An unremarkably featured white fellow of late middle age drove the carriage. The wagon was managed by an elderly Negro, his hair a snow-white wooly fringe around an otherwise gleamingly bald pate. The white man alighted, then with gesticulation and perfunctory command, it was clear he was ordering the old black to hoist my baggage into the wagon. Catching sight of Hattie, and having a few very brief words with her, he then drafted her into the endeavor as well, giving curt instruction that she was to assist the old man in his efforts.

I confess, seeing this preemptory treatment of noble Hattie by, what was to her, an absolute stranger, I had to suppress the urge to come to her defense with a demand for better treatment. But the realization of our current situation allowed me to restrain that impulse, though not the renewed twinge to my conscience as I watched her so menially used.

It took no great leap of intuition to understand that the white man must be some form of supervisor at Belle Bois. That being the case, and having discovered that Hattie was soon to be a 'fixture' of that plantation, he had considered himself well within his rights to employ her in assisting with the loading of her mistress's belongings for transport.

The disposition of my baggage attended to, the white man turned away and moved to join us in the Inn's foyer. His eyes fixed upon me almost from the moment of his progress through the door.

"Mist'us Katherine?"

I favored him with a slight inclination of my head. "I am she."

He quickly doffed a somewhat worn, but still very serviceable slouch hat, from his head, and returned my nod with a more respectfully deeper salute of his own. "I'm most powerful sorry 'bout all this here mix-up, ma'am. We di'n't 'spect y'all till day a'ter t'marrah, soonest."

Again Everett came to my assistance. "Katherine, this is Jeb Hawlsey, your overseer."

"Ah, Mr. Hawlsey. Well, no matter. I'm sure it couldn't be helped. That you're here and ready to undertake my conveyance is all that's really important."

I turned again to my dashing knight. "Everett, of course mere words can never repay your gallant deeds on my behalf tonight. I shall ever be in your deepest debt. Please, will you not do me the great honor of allowing me to offer small token of my gratitude and accept invitation to Belle Bois — shall we say, this coming Friday evening —for dinner? I should very much like to begin the renewal of acquaintance with my neighbors."

Here again, (and with secret amusement at the memory of the prank I had but recently perpetrated upon Captain Wickman at Justice Blanford's party,) I assayed to convey flustered infatuation for a man as, with downcast eyes, I completed my invitation by murmuring, "Especially the most valiant of my neighbors."

With effortless poise and grace, Everett raised my gloved hand to his lips, then replied, "Katherine, rest assured, the honor of your invitation and the opportunity to delight in more of your charming company is ample repayment for whatever humble service I could ever hope to attempt. I shall count the hours until Friday evening."

With a reprise of that tragically marred—yet strangely magnetic smile—of his, he took his leave.

****

My first morning at Belle Bois found me barely embarked upon my (as yet unfamiliar) day's routine when there came a soft tapping at my sitting room door. Opening it, I found a little black cherub no more than six years of age, he dressed in ragged trousers and a jersey top that was far too voluminous for his small frame. He gazed at me for a moment, his eyes large and filled with innocent inquisitiveness.

Crouching upon my heels, the skirts of the—hopefully businesslike and good-first-impression-engendering—dress gathering about me upon the floor, I smiled and in light tones inquired, "And who might you be, young master?"

The words must have provoked a wry frown upon my lips with the unintended inappropriateness of that appellation, for the little imp quickly averted his own gaze, adopting a downcast, subservient posture. His reply was whispered in a thin, reedy voice. "I's Adam, Mist'us."

Trying to make this lovely child more comfortable in my presence, I adopted a soothingly maternal tone and smiled, "Well then. Good morning to you, Adam. How fitting that you should be first to greet me in my new home, for shouldn't Adam always be the first?"

But the child only stared at his toes, still apparently quite over-awed by this audience with—

—his new owner.

"And what might your business be with me this morning?"

Again his mumbled reply was shyly offered to the floor, upon which the volume of my skirt flowed. "Missy Hattie say dere's somebody come up th' drive. White gen'el'man come a-callin'. She wanna know that this early in th' mornin', does you want ta meet him in th' parlor—or what?"

"A gentleman? What gentleman?"

But this was far out of little Adam's text. He could only shrug, his clear unease growing at his inability to meet his mistress's request for information.

I gave him a gentle pat on the head. "Well, never mind. I suppose I'll find out in short order, won't I? You go tell my Hattie that I'll receive our guest in the parlor. All right?"

Adam gave me a vigorous nod and, perhaps with no little relief, scampered off to deliver my imperial edict.

I watched his departing form with a sad little sigh. I needn't have taken that much concern for my attire this morning. I was Mistress of the Mansion now. All that I surveyed was, at the least, beholden to me; at the most, was my personal property. For all that my station elevated me above them, I could have appeared before my household attired in nothing but a nightdress; and still have dictated their every action with but a lift of my finger and a perfunctory command.

Others might find such power heady. I found it only made my unfamiliar surroundings, so far removed from my real home and my true nature, that much more alien and lonely.

Hearing a knock that was followed by someone being admitted below, I gave one quick glance in the glass to ensure that my disguise was unflawed, and then I descended to the ground floor and my unexpected guest.

I found him awaiting me, per my instructions, in the parlor just to the left of the main entryway. Having apparently heard the approaching swirl of my petticoats, he had already risen from the settee he must have only just sat upon, for he was standing as I passed through the curtained arch.

My first impression was that of a not-altogether successful tradesman. My guest was of small stature, but a few inches taller than my own disappointing height. But where I am slender, this fellow was portly. An ample stomach pressed against a waistcoat of indifferent quality. His face was fleshy and round, and his complexion was florid. A shock of carrot-colored hair rose in rebellious disarray above a receding hairline. The Derbyshire hat he nervously worked in both hands was neither stylish nor scruffy—a description that would describe his entire person when one thought of it.

I inclined my head in a little bow, and began: "Good morning, sir. Welcome to Belle Bois. Since I am the lady of the house, please allow me to introduce myself. I am Katherine Bonveneau."

I paused, expecting some return of introduction, but the little fellow only stared at me, his expression one of perplexed befuddlement. We stayed that way for an uncomfortably long moment, before I became disconcerted enough and forward enough to press my case. "Um, and you, sir. How may I be of service to you this morning?"

Fortunately, that was sufficient to snap his amazement, for he quickly stammered, "Oh! Ah, yes! Yes, Miss Bonveneau. Of course. Your servant—mistress. Your servant."

Still he stared at me much more closely than I felt appropriate. I had the sudden, shocking thrill of wondering if, somewhere along my progress from my rooms, something had come amiss in my facade and my masculinity was suddenly, in some way, glaringly obvious to this stranger.

Stifling the urge to run my hands over my hair and my person to check of discrepancies, (realizing that if anything was amiss, my sudden self-inspection would only make the situation that much worse,) I forced a calm, patient tone and asked, "By what name might I address you, sir?"

He shook his head as though to clear it from some disagreeable vision. "Ah! Reginald Digny, at your—oh, but I've said that, haven't I?"

That name—Of course! Niles' compatriot! The fellow who was to be my ally here, in my new situation.

I felt the tension of the moment begin to drain from me. "Mr. Digny, welcome! I hadn't looked for a visit from you, though, of course, such would be well advised and most timely. Please, sir, be seated. I think you and I have much to discuss, surely."

I had already taken several steps to the matching settee facing Digny's, when I realized that he was still standing there, unmoving, still staring at me in a most fixed and penetrating manner.

My glance prompted him to ask, in halting tones, "You—you did say you were Katherine Bonveneau, did you not? The—uh—the same Miss Bonveneau who is to take possession of Belle Bois?"

It was when I agreed, "I am she," that I finally began to suspect what might be the cause of this fellow's perplexity.

As I have said, my intention this morning had been to "dress to impress," as they say. To that end, I'd selected a smartly tailored gown in a handsome shade of forest green, with delicate white lace fretwork at breast and cuff. Upon rising, I had carefully donned the wig that Hattie had assisted me in styling into an attractively piled mass of lustrous light brown curls secured by a pair of matching jade green combs, one behind each ear. With my face powdered and subtly rouged, even I was impressed by the beauty that returned my gaze from the glass. Further, in that the dress I had chosen possessed a sufficiently revealing décolletage to warrant it, I was wearing the "heavier" of my two corselettes. Thus I presented to the world, and to my guest, more than a subtle hint at an enticingly fulsome bosom.

All of which finally gave clue, as I say, to the situation that now obtained.

I finally deduced that my disguise was far better than the good Mr. Digny had been expecting. He suddenly found himself in the awkward position of trying to decide whether or not the person he was addressing was the masculine compatriot in mischief whom he had been expecting, (though the outward show gave great lie to that proposition,) or whether the genuine Katherine Bonveneau had unexpectedly returned to Belle Bois, and his situation was suddenly become uncomfortably exposed and ambiguous.

For a moment, my roguish nature struggled for release, as I contemplated baiting this fellow by pretending that the latter possibility had indeed befallen. But ultimately, common sense prevailed and I contained myself allowing but this: I primly folded my skirts beneath me and daintily perched upon the settee.

Smiling a coy smile at the hands demurely folded upon my lap, in a most chaste voice I murmured, "I am indeed the Katherine Bonveneau you were expecting, Mr. Digny." Raising my eyes to his and allowing the true character of my smile to peek through the maiden's mask, I let a bit of slyness creep into my voice as I added, "Niles sends his regards. As does the good Captain."

His face now displayed the greatest degree of confusion, yet as he simply plopped down upon his settee and stammered, "But—but—the Miss Bonveneau I was expecting was a man!"

Turning an alarmed glance to the doorway, I hissed, "Hush, sir! Lower your voice!" Seeing only stalwart Hattie standing guard out in the foyer, I allowed my smile to return. With effort, I followed my own abjuration, lowering my own voice, both in pitch and in volume, before continuing. Forcing my voice into masculine tones, I growled, "Your expectations are not amiss. For I am indeed also a man."

Digny's expression was simply priceless. Remembering to cast his voice at a sufficiently conspiratorial volume he gasped, "Uncanny! Incredible! I—I—Niles had said your talents were not to be believed unless beheld firsthand, but—I had no idea!"

Returning to my artificial persona, I offered a coquettish giggle and a cooed, "Oh, how kind of you to say."

There followed another period where Digny simply (and rather rudely in any other circumstance) stared at me. Once again I was forced to nudge him into conversational motion. Continuing to play the role of callow lass struggling to rise to her station, I again smoothed my skirts and then, in businesslike tones, inquired, "So then, let us begin anew. To what do I owe this timely visit, sir?"

Once again, he shook his head as though to dispel some fantastic vision. "Ah! Yes, business. Well, I've come for two reasons today. The first, of course, was to make your acquaintance and to establish the fiction of attending to the transfer of your estate, from your late father's to your control."

I nodded. "Of course. That seems most natural and reasonable. Which reminds me, I never thought to ask, but surely at some point the genuine Miss Bonveneau will be wondering what is delaying the arrival of her proceeds from Belle Bois's sale. Since no sale is to take place, how are the funds. . .?"

Digny was settling into his element, the original shock of discovering my true nature now beginning to dissipate. He waved a hand in dismissal. "No fear there. The expected sum, and a bit besides, will soon be made good through the offices of Captain Wickman and his, um, 'superiors.' Miss Bonveneau should have no cause for complaint or suspicion along those lines."

This elicited another satisfied nod from me. "Excellent. Efficient, as I might have expected. I suppose that there will be papers and the like that will need attending upon, to promote the fiction of my assuming ownership?"

Digny nodded and patted a portmanteau that rested at his feet. "And I have them here. As I say, that very theme forms the excuse for my visit today. The first of many, I suspect. There will be a great deal of business to transact, thus allowing us to maintain a dialogue and thus support—um— our other 'affairs'."

Oh, dear, I'm such a rogue. At the word *affairs*, I surrendered to a wicked little impulse.

Arching my back just sufficiently to thrust that aforementioned bust into slightly greater prominence, I laid my left hand above the cleft of that bosom, fanned my face with my right, and pretended a coquettish fluster. " 'Affairs'? Why, la, sir! Do you propose to embark upon an alliance or a *dalliance?* To what straits would you force a poor maiden in her attempts to further her country's cause?"

The flame on Digny's cheek perfectly matched the fiery tinge of his hair as he stammered, "Madam! Or—or rather, Sir! Or—umm—"

I could contain myself no longer, and it was with a laughing voice that I again commanded, "Hush! Please, sir, do remember our danger and make at least some attempt to manage your tone. For my part, I'll try to manage my willful humor and not provoke you to further outburst."

Digny's chagrin melted into a sheepish smile as I continued, "Now, then. Did I not hear you say that the fiction of your service to Katherine as her attorney was but one of your reasons for today's visit? Is there more to transact?"

His smile grew positively wicked, and with an amusingly ill-fitting expression of deviltry upon that cherub's face, Digny leaned toward me and, after a theatrically broad glance about to ensure we remained private, whispered, "Indeed there's more—Nathan. I have a communiqué for you, smuggled into my possession after no little trouble and effort." Reaching down to that same portmanteau, he rummaged for a moment, then withdrew a much-folded piece of paper which he surreptitiously passed to me.

I gazed first at the paper in my hand, then at Digny, my eyebrow arching into a question.

After another furtive and unnecessary glance about, Digny confided, "From Niles. It's your first mission!"

IX.
The Iron Pumpkin

"But what am I to make of this?" I growled at Hattie. "How am I to proceed if I've no clue as to how to even make a start?"

That evening found me pacing to and fro about my sitting room, the skirts of my dress swirling about my ankles, displaying by their motion the agitation that their wearer sought to remedy.

With little success.

"Nathan, please—try to calm yourself," Hattie replied.

Hattie, as always, was the very picture of unruffled calm. Tonight, I found her placidity annoying.

"How? How shall I be calm when those that hold the course of my career propose to send me into harm's way with such poverty of guidance?"

Hattie maintained her equitable tone. "Surely, Niles and the Captain gave as much information as they thought prudent, given the tenuous nature of your line of communication."

I forced myself to cease pacing, seat myself on the edge of my bed, and at least try to appear as composed as the seemingly unflappable Hattie. "No doubt—no doubt," I said. "But that doesn't amend the situation we now find ourselves in. How are we to proceed on this—this—"

I could only wave my hand in frustration at the much-folded and well-traveled note that Digny had delivered. Hattie retrieved it from my bureau and perused it again, and for the —well, by this time I'd lost count of the number of attempts both of us had made to wring more meaning out of the terse missive.

Finally she sighed and set the note aside. "Well, I grant you that it is rather. . .scarce on detail."

My façade crumbled, and I bounded across to the bureau, snatching up the scrap of paper. " 'Sources indicate large quantity of rolled iron diverted to eastern S. Carolina. Investigate and report.' "

I slammed the paper down again. "Report about what? What do we know of rolled iron? How are we to begin to remedy our lack of knowledge? And should we discover anything, which I think is problematic at best, to whom do we report our findings? And by what method?"

Hattie sought for some answer but, as I feared, she could offer nothing of substance, and could finally only sigh and stare at her folded hands as she mused, "Well, for what is rolled iron used? How is it employed to further the Confederate war effort? For surely, that is the only usage that need concern us."

I tried to make something of this suggested line of thought, but failed. I threw up my hands. "Munitions, I suppose. Cannons. Musketry. Carriage fittings. Bah! Hardware of too many diverse descriptions to admit of easy catalog. The list is hopelessly large."

Hattie struggled for some retort, but could find none.

I resumed my agitated pacing. "All of this trouble and effort. All the hardship we endured getting here—the interminable sea voyage. That bone-jarring, rattletrap excuse for a railroad. The fracas at the terminal—"

Out of the corner of my eye, I saw Hattie suddenly sit upright in her seat, her eyes flying wide at some realization, and the beginnings of a smile gracing her lips.

I halted in mid-stride, and turned to glance over my shoulder at her. "Hattie?"

" 'What do we know of rolled iron?' We know that it's heavy, do we not?"

This line of thought took me by surprise. "Yes, that would seem a safe assumption."

"And how are large quantities of heavy commodities shipped throughout the South? Some goes by barge. I know, I still have memories of loading cotton bales upon them. But there is another conveyance. Might not the iron we seek even now be moving upon certain 'rattletrap railroads'?"

I began to see the glimmer of hope that clever Hattie's inspiration revealed. "Indeed. It seems that is a very likely possibility." Then the glimmer faded. "But what of that? How does the movement by rail of rolled iron bring us any closer to useful intelligence? We need to know where the iron is going, if we're to proceed. And how do we gather that knowledge? It's certain that we simply can't march into some shipper's office and baldly ask."

Hattie shook her head, her grin undiminished, my hope returning with that reassurance. "No. We can't ask about someone else's shipments. That's true. But Nathan, didn't you notice that when we embarked at Savannah, the unusually large number of goods wagons attached to the rear of our train?"

My chagrin at missing that salient fact must have been writ large upon my face, for Hattie didn't press the question. Instead, she simply forged ahead. "Well, there were. It's a sure thing that, with the war, the South's rail systems must be straining against the load."

I nodded. "Again, that seems a safe assumption. But how—?"

Hattie now had the bit in her teeth, and was proceeding at an enthusiastic mental gallop. "As with any overworked thing, Nathan: To find a hidden flaw, simply tax the system even further."

****

Mr. Hodge, the commissioner charged by the Confederacy's War Department with oversight of the rail network in and around Charleston, stared at me with undisguised disbelief.

"Pumpkins? You want to ship *pumpkins?*"

I nodded, my face set in a well-rehearsed little smile of girlish pride and accomplishment. "Indeed, sir. I have it on good authority that the cargo will require no less than three wagons of the type customarily used to transport produce. And all for immediate shipment, if you please. Halloween is not that far away, you know."

Hodge stammered with uncertainty. "But—see here, Miss Bonveneau. I can't—This is all very irregular."

I allowed a bit of uncertainty to cloud my countenance. " 'Irregular'? How so?" I turned and snapped my fingers, delivering a perfunctory command to Hattie who stood, subservient, her eyes downcast. (Struggling, no doubt, to conceal the twinkle of mirth that I knew danced in them.) At her cue, she quickly handed over the sheet of foolscap that I'd entrusted to her. "See here. I've drafted a complete listing of the points at which the cargo is to be loaded and the destination for each load, with due attention to the transshipment of each partial order. How can there be an irregularity—?"

Hodge waved his hands. "No, no! You don't understand. It's not where the cargo is to be collected, or where it's to be delivered. It's the actual moving of the —the pumpkins. The scheduling. There's the rub."

At this point, self-esteem drives me to declare that it took no little thespian ability for me to counterfeit the exact opposite of my true joy, and to force a deeper furrowing of my brow and a now-trembling voice as I murmured, "But why? I've—I've already purchased the pumpkins."

I resisted the urge to add a little sniffle to my performance, opting instead for subtlety. "Please, Mr. Hodge.

All my agents warned me that this was a mistake, but I was so certain! After all, in time of war, what could be more in demand than something to lift the spirits and bring gladness to the heart? Do you have no happy memories of carving a jack-o'-lantern on All Hallows Eve?"

"Why yes, but—"

"Then why will you not assist me in bringing that joy to our fellow countrymen in their time of need?"

Hodge's comical struggle to deal with the absurdity of this situation had Hattie biting her lip and pressing her chin against her chest to conceal her mirth. Fortunately, the usual obtained and Hodge had little interest in the doings of my 'nigger.'

All his attention was focused upon me, and upon the outlandish predicament I was thrusting him into. "Miss Bonveneau, you must understand. It's not that I'm unwilling to assist you. I—I like a good pumpkin as much as the next fellow."

Hattie's suppressed snort went unheard; and fortunately for me, I could contain my grin by a very natural biting of my lower lip, the same appearing to be a symptom of my increasing panic at the direction this discussion was taking. Hodge continued.

Hodges continued, "It's simply that there isn't excess capacity to move such a cargo on this short of a notice. I doubt that the capacity would exist, even without the exigencies of the War to contend with."

Now I did allow the sniffle, and more. "But—(sniffle)—I've already paid for them! For three carloads! Almost one hundred dollars' worth! Oh, Mr. Hodge—(sniffle)—what am I to do? They'll—(whimpering)—They'll be ruined if they aren't shipped! I'll—(sob)—I'll lose the entire price I paid, and—(sob)—and—"

Then I finally gave myself over to the outpouring of feminine woe that I've heretofore admitted is one of my strongest techniques.

Hattie, in a delightfully fitting turn, stepped forward and rubbed my shoulders. "Dere, dere, Missy Kate. Ever'thin' gwine work out fine in de en'. You see. We's gwine fin' a way."

Meanwhile, I was still making heart-wrenching sobs; but now I'd added twisting a dainty handkerchief in my lace-gloved hands.

Hodge would have been a cad indeed, if he could have watched this scene (well performed, if I do say so myself) and not have been moved to attempt some redress. "Oh dear— Now, please, don't carry on so, Miss Bonveneau. I'm sure that we—that *something* can be done."

I raised hopeful, tear-filled eyes to my rescuer. (Why should it be that it is so easy to counterfeit tears, yet so hard to feign a blush? Is that some comment on the natural state of Man?) "Oh—(sniffle)—Mr. Hodge! If you could but—(sniffle, dab at eyes)—oh, I'd be ever so grateful!"

"Of course, of course. Here, let me see that list of yours." I quickly passed the list that Hattie and I had spent the better part of a day concocting, across to my savior's hand.

He perused it for a moment, and you could see the alarm returning to his face at the complexity of the scheme proposed. I inserted another sniffle, and batted soulful, hopeful eyes at Hodge to forestall any further objection from him. Surrendering to the inevitable, he turned to a set of shelves behind him and withdrew a cloth-bound ledger, which he began to peruse.

It took the better part of an hour for all to be revealed.

Hattie and I had drafted the schedule of delivery of our pumpkins with an eye toward taxing as much of eastern South Carolina's rail system as was feasible. It was our dear hope that, being such a precious commodity to the agrarian South, the shipments of rolled iron would therefore be a priority. If, even after all the "incentive" that I had offered him, Hodge was still unable to override some previous movement of goods in favor of ours, it was our hope that this would be a clue to us that movement was a priority and that it might indeed be the rolled iron we sought.

Admittedly, this scheme was at best a rather thin gamble. But given the (presumptively) pressing nature of the time frame within which we worked, Hattie and I had been unable to devise any better ploy than this.

Providence must have been behind our endeavors, for as it transpired, our stratagem actually worked!

"This won't do, Miss Bonveneau. This movement via the Goose Creek Junction. That's simply impossible. Movement on that entire spur line is inviolate. I can't disrupt it."

Hodge had already made so many concessions by this point that I had to put a fairly brave face on the refusal. "Oh, dear. But that's such a large consignment. Surely you—?"

Hodge shook his head with absolute finality. "No, it's quite impossible. I simply can't interfere with the traffic on that route."

I took a slightly different tack. With a stamped foot and a childish (and hopefully fetching) pout, I again allowed a note of (this time, petulant) whimpering to color my words. "But whyever not? How mean you are not even to consider—Oh, please forgive me, dear Mr. Hodge. You've been so kind and helpful. Please don't believe that I'm ungrateful. It's just—you've been ever so clever in overcoming all other obstacles. What can be so important that you can't—?"

"I have no control over that line, don't you see? The military's shipments of iron take precedence over any other traffic. I have written orders to that effect, signed by the Secretary of War himself."

"*Iron?* My pumpkins are to be sacrificed for silly, cold lumps of iron?"

"Um, Mist'us?" Hattie said, looking worried.

I had pressed my case too hard. The darkening of Hodge's expression gave me ample proof of that. "Now see here, Miss Bonveneau! These shipments are surely for some crucial project, vital to the war effort. I'll thank you to bear that in mind!"

"Like what? What could be—?"

"I don't know, and you don't need to know, so why are you asking?" And now his eyes narrowed a little. *Suspicion.*

Realizing that I had played my cards to the extent of their worth, I folded my hands upon my skirts and nodded meekly, my gaze fixed on my toes. "Of course. Forgive me, sir. I'm being quite flighty and foolish, and I do sincerely beg your pardon. After all the assistance you've given me, it's positively churlish of me to scold and complain. I'm most genuinely sorry."

Hodge, of course, quickly softened his tone. "Why, not at all. Not at all. I quite understand your upset. I'm only too glad to be of assistance. But you must understand that in this particular instance, I'm quite powerless to help you. Surely you can see that?"

Hattie later told me that the smile Hodge received at that point was nothing less than angelic.

****

I said to Hattie, "Well, I'm duced if I can see why they would be shipping iron—or any other commodity, for that matter—to such an out-of-the-way spot."

Upon our return that evening to Belle Bois, Hattie and I had repaired to the study to see what conclusions we could draw from the intelligence our clever plot had garnered. My "father," (the late Mr. Bonveneau,) had amassed an enviable collection of maps and charts covering quite a large extent of the rural South. No doubt his cartographic collection was to aid him in his ancillary occupation as a traveling broker of agricultural goods. As his heir, I now made use of "Papa's" maps for an entirely different cause. I could only wonder what his feelings on the matter might be.

It had taken several moments of searching to locate "Goose Creek Junction" on one of the larger scale maps of Charleston County that we'd found neatly rolled and stored in a cabinet.

Once located and considered, both Hattie and I felt a less likely site for a vital military project could hardly be found.

Situated in a swampy area near where its namesake minor tributary joined the greater flow of the Cooper River, several miles removed from any sizeable habitation, the location seemed to offer nothing in the least attractive for any purpose other than breeding mosquitoes and cultivating Spanish moss.

Hattie tapped a finger on her chin and furrowed her brow. "Is there possibly some mistake? Are we looking in the right place?"

I indicated the map. "I doubt it. See here? It's clearly labeled. 'Goose Creek Junction.' You can see where the rail lines diverge. Surely there can't be more than one Goose Creek, let alone more than one Junction of the same name."

Hattie conceded the point. "But iron suggests industry. What possible industry could be situated in so remote a locale? And why?"

Nothing suggested itself to me, and I could only shrug.

Hattie continued, "Perhaps—a foundry? A munitions work? The easy access both to the Cooper River and thence to Charleston Harbor, and to the rail lines—?"

"That seems unlikely. Both river and rail are as easily accessed much closer and more conveniently to Charleston."

"True—true—"

We had the same thought at the same instant. It was I who gave it form. "Perhaps the isolated locale is desirable for just that reason: it is remote, and thus far from prying eyes and unwanted attention."

Hattie turned her dark, intelligent gaze my way and nodded. "That would explain much. But what, then, is the project that is being thus concealed?"

I gazed again at the map as though, by some divine inspiration, the secret might thus surrender to me. "There is but one way to answer that: We shall go and see."

X.
Moultrie

In any event, my intention simply to "go and see" proved much easier in the proposal than in the realization. What I had assumed would require but one afternoon's reconnoiter, in some suitably nondescript disguise, actually required several days' labor.

The morning following the enactment of our "Great Pumpkin Deception" found me bustling about (in my guise as Katherine, of course) attending to the thousand-and-one still-pending details attendant upon a major change of residence.

I had just completed a little charade in which I'd ordered the rearrangement of the sitting room's furnishings. (This for the third time, the completion of which returned the room's furniture to its original situation before any of the redecoration had begun.)

By chance more than design, the affair of the pumpkins had begun to establish the character of Katherine for me. For the betterment of that scheme, (the pumpkin deception,) I had found it beneficial to portray the flighty, scatterbrained little fluff-head. It had subsequently occurred to me that this persona might serve well to deflect suspicion over future "strangeness" and odd doings, and I determined to promote the fiction amongst the rest of my household and acquaintance.

As I say, I had thoroughly frustrated Jeb Hawlsey and a pair of the small corps of black field hands who serviced my estate with the meaningless rearrangement of some rather heavy furniture when the sounds of a rider approaching the grand entrance floated in through the open windows. Gazing out, I was somewhat surprised to see my beau, Everett Vincennes, riding up on a sturdy dapple-gray gelding.

As befitted my role, I quickly adjourned to the front portico to greet this unexpected arrival.

Proceeding through the front door, I anticipated encountering Everett ascending the steps, but instead I found him leaning down from his saddle, exchanging words with my majordomo, Old Tub.

(Old Tub was that same elderly Negro whom I had first beheld the night of my arrival at the train station. It was he who had been managing the wagon, the same fellow Jeb Hawlsey had been ordering about in the loading of my luggage. It later turned out that, of all my slaves, Old Tub was longest in service to the Bonveneau family, having originally "entered service" during the reign of my—or rather, Katherine's—grandfather. Grown old and tired after years in the fields, Tub's "reward" had been promotion to the Big House and employment as a domestic menial.)

Again, the swirl of petticoats attracted Everett's attention, for he glanced up from his discourse with Tub, his face assuming that smile I found so strangely attractive.

"Ah, Katherine. Good morning!"

With my right hand shielding my eyes from the brightness of what was a beautiful autumn morning, and my left hand pressed in commonly-feminine pose against the front, lower hem of my bodice, I returned Everett's smile with a genuinely warm one of my own.

(I found this undeniably courteous, genial, and stalwart individual truly impressive; and I was honestly eager to make more of his acquaintance. It is, to this day, a very real sadness that Fate prevented any relationship between us other than the fictional one we were allowed. I truly would have liked to be able to call Everett Vincennes a friend.)

"Everett, good morning! What a pleasant surprise! I was not expecting you until tomorrow evening. How nice to be able to welcome you today."

Instead of swinging down from his saddle as I would have expected a gentleman of his refinement to do, Everett instead sat upon his horse a bit straighter, his smile vanishing, his expression becoming instead one of disappointment.

"Your Friday invitation to dinner. Yes. I'm afraid that is the topic of my all-too-brief visit today."

I arched an eyebrow in interrogation; he continued: "Please forgive my haste, but I'm called away to duty. I fear I shall be quite occupied for the next several days, and therefore unable to attend upon you tomorrow night. Please accept my deepest regrets."

As I say, it required very little acting to portray my disappointment. "Oh, dear. Nothing seriously amiss, I hope."

He shook his head. "No. Not amiss. Rather, unexpectedly busy. I'm sorry, Katherine. I had quite looked forward to Friday."

I forced a smile onto my lips. "Well, there's little to be done for it, apparently. Duty to country must, of course, take preeminence. But might we not pick another date? One not too far in the future?"

His smile returned. "Ah, the very words I most hoped to hear. I would be delighted to accept such invitation. Might I be so forward as to suggest this coming Sunday? Indeed, might I be so terribly presumptuous as to offer to escort you to church? You'll be interested to know that Reverend Scoursby still shepherds our congregation."

I dropped my head, adopting my well-rehearsed coquettish smile, all to cover my fluster at having completely overlooked this (very necessary for a proper young lady) occupation: the attendance of Sunday services.

I murmured, "Now it is I who hear words most desired. I confess I have considered schemes by which I might wrangle just such an offer."

Lifting my chin a bit, from beneath heavy lashes I gazed at Everett and in coy tones confirmed, "You may escort me to church this Sunday. At what time will you call?"

Everett fairly beamed with pleasure. "Excellent! As services begin at eleven o'clock, shall we say ten? That will allow a leisurely pace, and the chance for a bit of conversation along the way."

I nodded. Propriety satisfied, I could again allow my smile free rein. "That would be most agreeable."

He dipped his head in a small bow. "And now, please excuse me, Katherine. I fear I'm already tardy for a morning full of demands."

I went so far as to bob a little curtsey. With the one strong hand remaining him, Everett reined his restive mount about, and proceeded back the way he'd come.

"Until Sunday, then," I called after his retreating form. His reply was a strangely jaunty wave of his crippled left arm as he disappeared out the gate.

As my mind was preoccupied with the demands upon my own time for this busy day, I quickly set thoughts of this coming Sunday with Everett aside.

Little did I anticipate that this seemingly unrelated meeting would figure so heavily in the affair I now turned to: a reconnaissance of Goose Creek Junction and the secrets that might be concealed there.

****

The first order of this day's business was to find some place where I might, in secrecy, go about the doffing of "Katherine," and the assumption of some other guise better suited to my nefarious intent.

It seemed prudent that I should undertake much of my activities in some guise other than Katherine. She was always to be my "safe harbor," the innocent, unsuspected mask behind which I could always retreat. Therefore, I desired, as much as possible, to shield her from any connection to my espionage activities. Especially, as was my present project, the more "active" endeavors.

So then, how to escape from prying eyes to safely effect my various metamorphoses? It was a surety that I could not effect the changes under the watchful eye of my household, without having them, in very short order, greatly suspicious of the many strange individuals who seemed to appear at the same times that "the Mistress" apparently vanished.

Fortunately, chance seemed to have provided a solution.

During my original whirlwind tour of my estate, I had espied, some distance from the Great House and secluded in a copse of elms, the rather dilapidated roof of a small outbuilding. Pointing to it, I had inquired of Jeb Hawlsey just what that building might be. He had replied that it was a disused storage shed, once housing tack and supplies for the adjoining fields, but subsequently abandoned in favor of a newer, more conveniently located facility (which, he then pointed out, at some remove across another field). Feigning disinterest in an unused shed, I'd continued with my tour. But in the back of my mind, I determined to later scout out this abandoned building as a possible staging area for my activities.

Upon the pretext of some business affairs to be transacted in Charleston, I gathered Hattie and a small valise purportedly containing documents for delivery to my attorney. In reality, the valise contained all things necessary for a suitable disguise I had devised.

Leaving Old Tub in charge of the household, and Jeb Hawlsey in charge of the fields, I took my leave for the afternoon.

With Hattie at the reins of my little pony trap, and I beside her upon the seat, we progressed at a leisurely pace down the tree-shrouded lane in the general direction of

Charleston. As we neared the weed-grown track that led, after passage through some fairly dense undergrowth, to that same disused shed, Hattie and I both carefully glanced about to ensure that our departure from our stated route would go unnoticed. Confirming that we were unobserved, we turned down the track and arrived, in short order, at our objective.

A quick examination proved that this outbuilding was indeed abandoned. Dilapidated and well layered with dust, it obviously had not been disturbed in quite some time. Nor did there seem to be anything of value amid the pile of cast-off miscellany that would call for a visit at any time soon by any member of my household.

In short, this building seemed ideally suited for my intended purpose.

With Hattie's aid, I quickly set about removing my wig, my powder and rouge, and the layers of clothing within which the prim and proper Katherine went about her day-to-day affairs. Having arrived at the ultimately intimate items of underdress, Hattie, as always, turned her back to grant me modesty as I finished disrobing.

Over her shoulder she inquired in conversational tones, "What personifications have you selected for our escapade?"

Donning the tattered trousers that formed fully half of the clothing of my chosen disguise, I replied, "Frankly, I had not given thought to any disguise for you. I had intended to make the initial foray alone."

There was a note of pique in her reply: "Why am I to be excluded?"

I pulled on the shabby vest that went with the trousers, and replied, "Because, frankly, while this disguise seems suitably anonymous and unsuspicious, I could think of no matching persona for you to adopt that would be likewise anonymous and unsuspicious."

Deciding that I had donned sufficient clothing that she could safely view me and still leave my modesty intact, Hattie turned about, and gazed at the already well-advanced assumption of my latest impersonation. She raised an eyebrow, not yet comprehending what it was she beheld.

It took no little quantity of earth from the floor of the shed, liberally applied about my face and person, and my immersion into the role before Hattie finally grasped the character I intended. But once all was complete, her sharply insightful judgment was well satisfied with the quality of my disguise.

As we were departing the shed en route to Goose Creek, it was Hattie who had a sudden inspiration for the augmentation of my characterization. She described her intent to me and I quickly endorsed the addition, thinking it quite clever at the time.

We spent several minutes rooting about in the detritus of the shed before we found a suitable item to fulfill Hattie's inspiration.

****

I shifted the rather heavy wooden box under my arm, placing my other fist on my hip in insolent challenge.

"Lookee here," I growled, in a—suitable for my apparently tender years—adolescent pipe. "I 'uz told I'd get a dollar fer totin' this here doodad alla way from Summerville. So, I sez ag'in that if'n you wants it, you pony up a dollar. And that's flat!"

The more burly of the two guards, the one with the bristling black beard that fell well down his chest, glowered at me. "An' I sez that I don' care what you wuz tol'. If'n that box goes here, you han' it over and be on yer way."

I spat on the ground at my feet (as befit the character of the ne'er-do-well young layabout I pretended to be.) "I won't neither. Not lessen you—or him"—here I indicated the small, sallow associate of the first guard—"or *somebody* gives me th' dollar I's owed!"

Now that same pallid individual spoke. "Who wuz it tol' ya ta bring that thing here?"

I gave an insolent shrug. "Some jasper sittin' 'hind the winder down ta the Summerville railroad station. Don't know his name. But he sez if'n I tote this here box fer him, somebody here'd pay me a dollar ta do it."

The guards exchanged a sour glance. It was the beefier of the two who growled, "That Willard, I swear! He's so lazy he'd not budge his a___ ta fetch a bucket if'n his hair wuz on fire!"

(So! Willard is your name, eh? Well, Mister Willard—perhaps the trouble this little incident might cause for you will teach you to be more industrious about your labors! Particularly in the assistance of poor young women who come to you for succor in their time of distress, as one did but one week past, and you could not even trouble yourself to rise from your stool to point out the way to the local hotel!)

As the discussion of Willard's lack of industry was not progressing my intent in any meaningful way, I pressed my case. "So. What's it ta be? Does I gets mah dollar, or does I take this here box alla way back ta Summerville an' one o' y'all can stir yerselves ta come an fetch it?"

The large guard glared at me. "You watch that back-sass, you young pup. Lessen you wants ta learn better manners at the end o' my belt!"

I was about to deliver some scathing reply when the approaching beat of several sets of hooves finally impinged on my awareness. Indeed, by the time my attention (so fixed upon my characterization and the exchange of "pleasantries" with the guards) was finally penetrated by this new occurrence, the quality of the noise indicated that at least one rider must have approached very close behind me before I was actually aware of him.

Turning about, I received the shock of my life as I gazed up at the rider who was, indeed, but scant feet away from me.

A rider who sat erect and dignified in his saddle.

A saddle on a sturdy, dapple-gray gelding ridden by a tall, commanding fellow.

A fellow with a cast covering a jagged scar and a missing left eye; and whose left arm hung stiffly, lifelessly at his side.

Everett Vincennes.

For a horrible, infinitely drawn-out moment, I was quite certain that the disdainful stare he aimed at me was for his sudden realization of the deception that had been perpetrated by the now-recognized spy standing before him, gaping up at him as "she" had but a few hours ago, there in the lane before the house she had usurped.

His words were an imperious rumbling: "What's this then? Why is this young rascal standing here at the checkpoint? What's his business?"

At the blessedly-welcome word *his*, I found I had sufficient presence of mind remaining to drop my head, now hopefully unrecognized for its shock of (unfamiliar to Everett) short-cropped and dark brown hair, upon a chest now obviously masculine beneath its threadbare vest.

The sallow guard spoke: "He sez he's got some parcel from the Summerville rail station ta deliver, Major, suh."

Everett grumbled. "A parcel? What parcel?"

The burly guard prodded me in the back and snarled, "You give that box ta the Major, and be sharp about it!"

Trying to avoid exposing my visage as much as possible, I passed the small wooden crate up to the Major, which he, with some difficulty, finally managed to grasp in his good right hand by pressing the box against his prosthetic left forearm. After a bit of struggle, he managed to pry off the lid and peer inside. Now his tone was more befuddled than anything else. "What the duce is this supposed to be? What need have we of some rusty cog?"

At the time, Hattie's suggestion that I supply myself with some boxed "cargo," as a dupe by which I might bluff my way past any security for the Goose Creek site, had seemed like such an excellent idea. Now, in hindsight, the stratagem of carrying a cast-off bit of debris, which we'd found amid the shed's trash, as passport, and of demanding an outrageously princely sum for its surrender if challenged, seemed ludicrously ill-advised and perilous.

With my face still downcast, I could but shrug and in as soft a voice as I thought prudent, mumble, "Don' know, suh. They jes' tol' me ta tote it here."

Amazingly, the heavier-set guard offered, "That good-fer-nothin' Willard tol' the boy somebody here'd pay him a dollar fer the job."

From the corner of my downcast eye, I saw Everett toss the box and its contents to the pallid guard. "See that Wainwright gets that. Perhaps he'll know what to do with it."

Then, gentleman that he was, Everett fished in the pocket of his waistcoat for a moment, before withdrawing a silver coin, which he flicked to me. "There, boy. One dollar, as promised."

The next moments are still clearly, indelibly etched in my mind.

I looked up, the better to snatch the coin from the air. At that instant Everett got his first, good look at my now-upturned face and I was sure I caught some glimmer—well, if not of recognition, at least of puzzlement—dawning there. The coin successfully caught, I again turned my head away in preparation of a hasty retreat. As I did, my eyes passed across the conveyance of the individual accompanying Everett.

There, slightly behind and to the left of Everett was a small carriage drawn by a single horse. In it sat a single man.

Before I dropped my head and departed at a fairly brisk trot, I beheld his face.

If encountering Everett had been a shock, at least it was, in retrospect, not altogether unexpected. But I'm sure that at sight of the face of this second person—a person who gave added wings to my flight, lest I somehow be betrayed through recognition by yet another person from my past—my jaw must have gaped wide in absolute amazement before I dropped my head and fairly bolted from the scene.

For there, sitting in the carriage with a look of bored disinterest on his face, was the same inexperienced youth Katherine had taken such great delight in teasing during their shared passage aboard the *Elsie Boone—*

James Eddiborogh.

XI.
Feminine Wiles

The tension of that terrible moment, when I had stood there, positive that my deception was on the verge of penetration, positive that all was about to be undone, and my life would surely be forfeit for the discovery, knotted my stomach with suppressed panic all the way back to my rendezvous with Hattie (where she held our pony trap concealed within a grove of trees at some remove from the roadblock we had espied, only just in time to prevent our own notice as we'd blithely proceeded down the lane leading to the Junction).

Hattie must have read my disconcert, for her greeting was a worried, "Nathan, has something come amiss?"

Standing bent at the waist, my hands upon my knees as I struggled for breath, I finally managed to relate, between gasps, what had transpired at the checkpoint. Her expression became at once troubled and thoughtful.

"Vincennes? Of course. We should have anticipated that eventuality: that the commander of the militia would have charge of whatever security measures would be in place for the safeguarding of their secrets. But *James Eddiborogh?* What possible connection could he have with any of this? Now, more than ever, we need to gain admittance to that place. Mysteries are piling up too high—"

I had finally recovered sufficient breath after my mad dash, to forcefully interrupt her ruminations. "*Are you crazy as a loon?* After such a near-escape as that, I'll be d___ned if I ever stir one foot closer to that place!"

Hattie, for the very first time, displayed some anger of her own. "Nathan! Really, calm yourself. Had you truly been suspected of anything, you would have been detained and questioned, not simply allowed to scamper away."

I forced myself to reconsider. Had I truly seen suspicion and dawning recognition on Everett's face?

Or, as I now reconsidered, had all been the product of a suddenly overwrought imagination?

Surely, Hattie was correct. Had I been suspected, I would have been detained.

Yet—Everett's expression as I snatched the coin—

I chewed my lip and cast a troubled glance over my shoulder in the direction I'd just come. "I don't know. Perhaps—"

Hattie laid a comforting hand on my shoulder. "Rest easy, Nathan. I didn't mean that we should make another attempt now. I agree we'd be tempting fate at this point, suspicions or no, to make some other effort this soon."

To my shame, I admit I readily nodded and agreed with Hattie's wise prudence. Though it was not for wisdom displayed, but for release from dread, that I did.

****

It was as Hattie was lacing up Katherine's corset, (her "ordinary" corset, not the already-concealed beneath chemise and shift "corselette",) there in the disused shed as we prepared to return to Belle Bois, that I felt her deft fingers pause. I sensed a distraction in Hattie.

The turning of my head over my shoulder was sufficient to recapture her attention. With thoughtful tones, she murmured, "Perhaps it is unnecessary for you to set foot toward the Goose Creek Junction after all. At least for the moment. Perhaps—"

At the happy thought that this dangerous, now deeply disturbing occupation might be avoided for a time, I said, "Tell me, what have you devised?"

With serious mien, she cautioned, "Don't be so eager until you have heard what I propose. For it may well be more perilous than simply walking up to the gates of whatever installation lurks beyond the checkpoint and boldly demanding to know what transpires there."

I frowned, I'm sure. "What? What could be more perilous than that, or that I'd consider your new inspiration, given the danger you seem to think is inherent?"

Hattie's answer was a strange non sequitur, "How many roads lead from Goose Creek back toward Charleston?"

Having by now become used to Hattie's oddly disjointed, but ultimately productive method of reasoning out the solution to a problem, rather than asking what that had to do with anything, I pondered the question for a moment.

Remembering "Papa's" maps, I replied, "Well, for the first several miles there is but the one route—the Old Post Road—that leads directly between the two. Of course, one also might go roundabout via the Ladsonville Pike or, alternately, west then south via—"

Hattie waved a hand to silence me. "No. I think we need only concern ourselves with that one direct route."

I saw no enlightenment in this, and finally voiced my confusion. " 'Concern ourselves' in what way?"

But Hattie was lost in her mental convolutions. After a long, long moment of consideration, her reply was to give me a most piercing stare and a thoughtful, "Yes. . .yes, I think you could do it, Nathan."

I relaxed—until Hattie continued: "But unless I miss my guess, before all is done, it will surely become the most challenging performance you've ever given. Pray to God it works—and that we both survive it."

****

The sun was well advanced down the sky, and evening was fast approaching, before we could put Hattie's grand scheme into motion.

Twice her call from her vantage point as lookout upon the brow of the little hill had set me scrambling to conceal the pony and cart within the empty, roadside barn we'd selected for concealment, lest some unrelated-to-our-design traffic encounter the scene we intended, and thus ruin our device.

But her third call, coming almost at the point where I was about to suggest that we abandon the attempt for this day, given the lateness of the hour, was the agreed-upon two short whistles that indicated the approach of our quarry.

With haste I led our shaggy little pony, still tethered to the cart, once more out of the barn and stood him in the lane. Poor brute, he gave me a look that I swear conveyed impatience at the foolishness he simply couldn't fathom— the charade that led him back and forth from road to barn, (a barn quite bereft of any of the expected comforts of manger or familiar stall,) to no apparent purpose other than fulfilling some inscrutable whim of his incomprehensible human masters.

I then picked up a stone, raised his right foreleg, and proceeded to lodge the rock in that tender area of flesh above and within the insensate horn of his hoof. This served only to add injury to the insult that had heretofore comprised the poor, patient creature's afternoon.

At the sudden discomfort, he whickered once and attempted to shy away. But when his now disabled leg struck the ground, he began to lamely dance about, with even more distress as the pain of the lodged stone now made itself felt. I grabbed him by the head and tried to gentle him, murmuring my genuine regret at his necessary discomfort, and my sincere pledge that, if all went well, his torment would soon end.

Hattie's dash from her place of concealment brought her beside me just in the nick of time. No sooner had she arrived than Everett, astride his dapple gray, and the carriage bearing James hove into sight, as the two men made their way back to Charleston after a day of—

Whatever occupation claimed their attention at the Goose Creek facility.

The occupation that I was now determined to discover, through implementation of Hattie's clever—but admittedly dangerous—plan.

Forcing aside my sudden dread at another encounter with Everett this soon after the fright of the meeting at the checkpoint, I instead feigned a smile of relief and cried, "Everett! Oh, thank goodness! Help!"

Reining up beside us, he stared down at me from his saddle; and I added my now-genuine relief to my characterization. I was relieved that Everett's gaze on me was completely unsuspicious and showed only concern. Everett asked, "Katherine? What's wrong?"

I stroked our restive pony's head and whimpered, "The poor brute's come up lame somehow. He simply refuses to take another step. I feared my Hattie and I would be marooned here until darkness fell. Thank Heaven you've chanced by!"

As Everett dismounted to examine our horse, from the corner of my eye, I saw other movement that I correctly deduced indicated that the occupant of the carriage was also proceeding to my aid.

The surprised voice quickly confirmed my deduction.

"Katherine? Katherine Bonveneau?"

I glanced up with a look of surprise, as I pretended for the first time to recognize the face. "James Eddiborogh? Whatever are you doing here?"

His face was a study in happy confusion. "Why, I've been retained by the Government to attempt my new methods for *Moultrie*."

It took all of the skill I possessed not to pounce upon this enticing revelation, and instead pretend only mild interest. I folded my hands upon the volume of my skirts and sought to match James' smile with one of my own. "Moultrie? Who is that?"

James was on the point of replying when a loud interruption from Everett prevented James from answering: "Here's your trouble, Katherine. Your horse has a stone lodged in his hoof. No doubt the quick is bruised and that's the cause of his refusal to proceed."

Forcing back frustration at coming so close to my goal, only to be thwarted as the words were about to leave James' lips, I turned a look of wide-eyed concern (the best I could contrive to conceal my pique) upon Everett. "Oh, dear! Poor thing! What's to be done?"

Straightening from his crouch, Everett used his right hand to dust off the knees of his breeches, then considered for a moment before replying, "Well, since Belle Bois is not that far distant, I'd propose that you join Mr. Eddiborogh in his carriage. We can set a leisurely pace as your servant follows along behind, leading your pony."

Very well. I had been thwarted in an easy procurement of the information I sought, but I was hardly defeated. Nodding assent at Everett's suggestion, I allowed the next stage of Hattie's grand design to unfold: the seduction of James Eddiborogh.

****

There followed a series of introductions wherein it became apparent to Everett that I already knew James, and to James that I was previously acquainted with Everett. Once introductions were complete, James, with blush and fluster as his hands encircled my waist, assisted me up upon the carriage seat.

With Everett remounted and pacing his dapple along beside the carriage, and Hattie trudging along behind, leading our still limping pony, we proceeded toward Belle Bois.

Since I thought suitable conversation had passed, such that I might again address the topic and not seem overeager, I turned to James and in light tones enquired, "But, you were saying something about. . .'Morrisey', was it?"

He chuckled. "Not 'Morrisey'. *Moultrie*. That is her name."

I arched an eyebrow. " 'Her'? You have been engaged into the service of some woman?"

Another chuckle. "It might well be said that I have. And a beautiful woman she is! I saw her for the first time not three hours hence as she laid in her—"

Everett's normally handsome voice was again a rude interruption. "Mr. Eddiborogh, perhaps you should take some thought—?"

But this time I was not to be denied, for I had a perfect excuse to override the Major's interruption. With an expression that proclaimed scandalized propriety, (while simultaneously hinting at secret, wicked interest,) I interrupted with, " '*As she laid in her*'—goodness! James, how scandalous! What have you been about?"

Ignoring Everett completely, with a huge grin James answered. "I was about to say, 'as she laid *in her moorage*.' *Moultrie* is a ship, Katherine! To be precise, she is *C.S.S. Moultrie*. And I have been engaged to be her pilot."

The note of stern rebuke in Everett's voice was now becoming dangerous. "Mr. Eddiborogh, enough! Remember the need for discretion!"

Everett's tone finally penetrated, and James turned a chastened expression in the Major's direction. "But surely there's no harm in telling Katherine? What possible danger—?"

Portraying girlish glee at the prospect, I pressed one hand against my bosom and giggled, "Is this some *secret?* Oh! How delicious!"

Thinking to deflect suspicion by proclaiming the very thing, I next folded my hands on my lap and glanced from beneath lowered lashes at the two gentlemen, as I attempted a feigned look of sinister triumph (hoping the same appeared laughably inappropriate on my innocent, open features.) "Excellent! My nefarious plan progresses! Soon I shall know all!"

James' renewed chuckle indicated that my act was producing the desired effect, at least upon him. But when I glanced in Everett's direction, to my disquiet I again beheld that expression of—incipient recognition? Puzzlement?

"Katherine," Everett sighed, that fleeting expression replaced by quiet concern. "It's not a matter for play or jest. Mr. Eddiborogh had disclosed something to you that really should have been kept more discrete."

Now I laid into my characterization of the little fluff-head with a will. "Oh Everett! Don't be such a goose! Of course your secret is safe with me."

Here I contrived a look of sudden puzzlement. "Whatever that secret might be."

Then I brightened with the happy knowledge that I now possessed a bit of some shared confidence, understood or not. "I'll have you know that of all of the girls at school, it was well known that Katherine Bonveneau could always to be trusted with any confidence, no matter how tempting in the revelation it might be. Why once, I recall how positively torturous it was to stay silent after Chastity Fox whispered to me of her scandalous infatuation with—" The sly smile returned to my lips, as I again folded my hands primly in my lap. "But, that would be telling, wouldn't it?"

Then I simply sat, smug in the proof of my trustworthiness as James continued to grin (now fondly?)

and Everett simply chewed his lip and looked more troubled than ever.

Realizing that any further prying would surely excite more suspicion on Everett's part than I could deflect, instead I turned the topic to something else entirely.

Or so I hoped it seemed at the time.

"Oh! I've a sudden thought! James, the Major has offered to escort me to church this Sunday. Please, won't you come too? Indeed, we are then to share Sunday dinner together at Belle Bois and it would be ever so grand if you could join us for that as well. Oh, please say you will! We have so much to catch up on, and I have such amazing stories to relate about my adventures since we parted company in Savannah!"

James was already nodding enthusiastically before I'd completed even half of my invitation. "Oh, yes! Oh, Miss Bonveneau, I'd be most delighted to accept your invitation! How wonderful!"

Another giggle, a hand laid gently, tentatively atop James' as he held the reins and a winsome glance at Everett completed my distraction from the dangerous topic of secrets divulged. It was interesting to note that Everett's frown had changed its character a bit, or so I would have wagered. Still thoughtful, still troubled, I wondered if now I didn't detect just a note of—jealousy?—there as well.

*****

Believing that I had sufficiently tempted fate for the moment, I undertook nothing further to advance my intelligence-gathering activities the following day (Saturday), opting instead to dash about in my now well-recognized dither as I chivvied my servants through premature preparations for the upcoming feast.

Under the pretext of planning my wardrobe for the morrow's festivities, Hattie and I retired to my chambers a little after two o'clock, with instructions that I was not to be disturbed for any but the most dire emergencies.

Safe within the shelter of my boudoir, Hattie and I considered the possible significance of what we had learned to date.

Hattie sat at my dressing table, thoughtfully stroking her chin. "So, this all revolves around a ship, does it?"

Seated in my accustomed place upon my bed, I nodded. "Indeed. But that being the case, what are we to make of this large quantity of rolled iron? What has that to do with ships?"

Hattie glanced up, her expression displaying mild frustration at my ignorance. "Why, Nathan—it is to be an ironclad, obviously."

I beg the reader to remember that at this time (the autumn of 1862) ironclad warships were still very much a novelty, the seminal battle of *Monitor* versus *Merrimac* (or *Virginia*, as she was styled in the South) having taken place but some sixth months previously. Of course, my disinterest in the War that obtained at the time also contributed to my lack of enlightenment on the topic.

" 'Ironclad'? What's that?"

Hattie sighed. "It's a novel method by which—well, I suppose a ship is either provided in some way with attached iron plating, or—I'm unsure, perhaps they even build the ship out of iron to begin with. In either event, it produces, by all accounts I've read, a most formidable floating weapon."

I nodded, contriving to look at once sagacious and concerned. "Ah! That business. Of course."

Unlike James Eddiborogh, Hattie was not taken in one whit by my performance. She simply raised an eyebrow, her disillusioned frown perhaps a bit overdone to convey her feelings. I was reduced to a sheepish grin and a little shrug.

Hattie forged ahead. "In any event, it's clear that we now have something to report. Something quite important."

Now it was my turn to frown. "Report? No we won't!"

Hattie reared back in surprise at my sudden vehemence. I moderated my tone. "I mean that surely we won't report this scarcity of intelligence, that our sole discovery is the building or modification of some ship. Surely there's a great deal more to uncover before we risk sending a communication northward."

Hattie clearly was unconvinced. "Nathan, I think we've pressed our luck as far as is prudent, and perhaps a bit further. Did you not see the expression on Vincennes' face while James was spouting his confidences, which you were so eager to gather up? There is doubt beginning to tickle the Major's conscience. Better we leave well enough alone and divorce ourselves from anything further, lest that tickle become something more tangible. Do not forget how perilous is our situation, how close to the brink we tread, even when we do nothing but sit upon our hands."

Tucking those hands within arms that I folded in display of determination beneath my ersatz breasts, I dropped any pretense at feminine tones to proclaim, "I disagree. I judge this to be a once-in-a-lifetime opportunity, not to be missed through timidity. Eddiborogh is apparently willing enough—no, *eager* or I'm no judge—to divulge a whole plethora of secrets, if by so doing he will increase his stature in the eyes of the woman who holds his infatuation. We shall seize this opportunity."

Hattie was about to voice some further objection, but relented at my obviously set determination. Dropping her gaze she murmured, "Very well, Nathan. As you think best."

I wish that I could say this was the last time I ever overrode Hattie's impeccable judgment to my subsequent discomfit. Worse yet, I wish that I could say it was I who paid the price for my overweening pride and self-assurance, and not she.

As, in this case and before all was said and done, the cost of that price ultimately befell.

****

Sunday dawned as bright and clear as the days that had gone before. At the appointed hour of ten o'clock, a stylishly appointed brougham turned into our lane with a liveried Negro at the reins. In it sat Everett, dashing in his Major's uniform (complete with plumed hat), and with James well-attired in a handsome ensemble of navy-blue serge. I greeted my escort at the portico, arrayed in my finest gown of plum-colored satin, with its modestly high collar of lace flounce, and its generously wide hoop-skirts that floated and swayed with a whisper of silk and crinoline at each dainty, slipper-shod step.

With decorous modesty, I dipped a full curtsey, brushing back the veil that completed my costume, the better to smile my welcome to these two handsome beaus.

"Gentlemen, good morning! And isn't it a lovely one?"

As befit good manners, both stalwarts alighted and ascended the steps to take my greeting. Everett, senior of the two, was the first to take my hand. "Katherine, indeed it is! More radiant still, for the beauty its gentle light reveals."

Oh, for the ability to blush at will! I had to content myself with a quick, demure drop of my eyes and an (intentionally) ill-concealed smile of pleasure at this enchanting compliment.

James next took my offered hand and gave good attempt to match Everett's easy charm. "Indeed, you're a feast for the eyes today, Miss Bonveneau."

Remembering in which direction my ultimate objective lay, I turned my full attention upon James and cooed, "With a dashing gentleman to admire her, any girl would be radiant. Beauty is in the perception, Mr. Eddiborogh."

Everett sought to reclaim my attention. "I disagree, Miss Bonveneau. This morning delights in a loveliness that is surely objective, and needs no *flattery* to sustain itself before the world."

Well, that was simply too good not to acknowledge; and I, perforce, decided that my best course would be to divide my charms between these two. On the one hand, the better to obtain the information I sought, on the other, to deflect such suspicion as might still linger.

With the pleasantries of greeting attended to, I was assisted into the carriage and the three of us set off for the church.

The ride progressed in amiable fashion with light, inconsequential chat about the weather and other matters. I studiously avoided any mention of the *Moultrie* or of James' or Everett's connection therewith.

*****

It was when we were perhaps halfway to our destination that a singular event occurred, which in retrospect takes on even more meaning than I then attached to it.

We were passing down a tree-shrouded lane approximately halfway between Belle Bois and Everett's plantation when he pointed to a large oak tree set some little distance back from the road. "Oh, Katherine, look there. Do you remember the adventures we had as children in the limbs of that stout old fellow?"

I was about to fabricate a smile for some nonexistent memories of a (for me) fictitious childhood romp, when, from the corner of my eye, I caught what I thought to be a strange light in Everett's eye that didn't quite match his charming, easy smile.

"Um, in that tree? Oh, my—Everett, please forgive me. Of which adventures do you speak?"

His expression surely spoke of disappointment. Didn't it?

"Katherine, can you have forgotten? Has it been that many years that I have been out of your thoughts? Do you not recall the time when, at your behest, I essayed to climb to the uppermost limb, and for my pains got nothing but a broken crown and a broken arm when my competence at tree climbing proved sadly less than my aspiration?"

I joined in James' smile at the image this invoked, making sure to add a touch of embarrassment at my inability to summon "the memory."

"Dearest Everett, please forgive my shockingly faulty recollection. I don't know how I could have lost such a memory as that. Please think it is but the passage of too many trying years following my separation from home and company that is the cause, and not any failure of my esteem for you."

My excuse was, of course, readily accepted. (It being far too boorish for Everett to have pressed the issue, given my intimation at the hardships composing my mythical youth as my excuse.)

The rest of the journey passed without further incident. But the doubt I now entertained as to Everett—what might have been the result if I had feigned a delighted memory for an event that may *or may not* have actually occurred— lingered close behind my smile and sparkling laughter.

****

Of course I was the toast of that morning's services, as all of the local gentry took the opportunity to get a good look at the newly installed Mistress of Belle Bois. I'm quite sure my performance of that role, both during the services and after, as a seeming-thousand introductions were exchanged on the steps of the church, was in all quite serviceable and readily accepted by everyone.

James too received his share of inspection as the community's most recent visitor. Though I was attentive for any dropped snippet of information that might have emerged as a result of James' introduction, I was disappointed in my hopes, for nothing more did I learn of any use.

After the service, I overheard Reverend Scoursby murmur to Everett in a low voice, "Is my memory playing tricks? I thought her hair was more blonde than that."

Everett replied in an even quieter voice; I could not hear what he said.

****

Returning to Belle Bois, I was again assisted from the carriage, and both of my gallants took my leave with professions of their eagerness for that evening's festivities.

I adjourned to my rooms to while away the few odd hours before it was time to begin dressing for dinner.

And to ponder the significance of that morning's occurrence.

****

The dinner party that evening was, for the most part, quite enjoyable and uneventful.

Everett and James arrived a little after 6 p.m., again sharing Everett's carriage. Again, both were most impeccably turned out in the most fashionable of eveningwear.

I greeted them in the grand foyer, likewise most suitably attired in a formal gown of peach-colored satin. A gown that took advantage of the evening hour and allowed my two gentleman callers an enticing exposition of beguilingly bare shoulder and bewitching bosom. The memory of Everett's troubled expression during our meeting at the checkpoint was still fresh, and I was determined to cloud the waters with seemingly irrefutable proof of femininity.

As befit good manners, each of my guests had brought a gift; in Everett's case, a magnum of fine wine, in James' case, a mixed bouquet of autumn flowers. Remembering where my better hopes lay, and again to perhaps discomfit Everett, (that little twinge of jealousy was also remembered,) I gathered James' flowers into my arms and moaned with pleasure as I drank in their perfume. "Oh, James, how enchanting! Such loveliness!"

Turning to Hattie, (who stood to one side, unobtrusive in her drab maid's livery,) I handed her the flowers with the instruction, "Find a vase for these and see that they grace our table tonight."

She bobbed a little curtsey. "Yes'm, Mist'us Katherine."

Almost as an afterthought, I also passed across the bottle of wine—without comment.

As I say, there was no little apprehension on my part that Everett might take this occasion for further probes of my "memory," but such was not the case. At least I have no recollection of any overt test of my bona fides. Rather, the evening was, as I say, quite mundane and pleasurable.

But for two items of note.

After an excellent repast of fish, (procured that morning by Hattie while the gentry had been attending church,) complemented by the bounty of my kitchen garden, Everett, James and I, (with Hattie in attendance as chaperone,) adjourned to the salon where the gentlemen might imbibe some of "my father's" stock of brandy, and I might enjoy their conversation.

Of my impersonation of Katherine to date, this episode was, in fact, quite the easiest. There was actually little for me to do but sit, idly toy with my fan, and pretend a childish infatuation with these two (truly) charming individuals as they recounted interesting anecdotes, or attempted to best each other with adventures they had had over the years. Needless to say, Everett quickly outstripped James in the latter category. And though the topic of military service did, of course, arise, by some unspoken mutual understanding, the topic of Everett's injuries was not broached. (I might mention that my original gambit of favoring James with the bulk of my attention, first employed in the matter of gifts, but subsequently pursued throughout the evening, worked as I had hoped. Everett did indeed seem to be more interested in procuring my favor than in testing my identity, as his continuing domination of the conversation proved.)

In any event, it was perhaps a little after eight o'clock when I heard some small commotion out in the entranceway. I was about to dispatch Hattie to investigate when young Adam, (who would have been trembling in his boots—had he had any—at the solemnity of the occasion and august nature of the personages upon whose presence he intruded,) peeped through the drawn curtains. In a—comical for its absolute failure to be surreptitious—whisper he hissed, "Missy Hattie! Dere be some soljur outten de lane. He say th' Major's suppos' ta come quick!"

All of us smiled fondly at Adam's innocence and seriousness, and Everett rose with, "If you'll pardon me for but a moment, Katherine?"

As soon as he was gone, the second singular event occurred when James, in a most conspiratorial manner, leaned toward me and asked, "If I might be so bold, what it your schedule for tomorrow, Katherine?"

I had no idea what might be in the offing, but I sensed an opportunity and took it. "Why, I had no especial plans. Simply more of the drudgery of arranging my new household."

James grinned. "Excellent! Would you perhaps be interested in a bit of a diversion?"

I returned his smile. " 'Diversion'? Why, whatever are you proposing, Mr. Eddiborogh?" This, accompanied by the coy press of folded fan to breast, and coquettish lowering of smiling eyes.

"Might I not invite you to a little adventure upon the river tomorrow?"

Before I could reply, we heard Everett's voice from the entranceway giving someone orders to "Attend to that, and I shall be along presently."

James' hissed, "Benbow's Landing. Tomorrow morning at ten. Please say nothing to Vincennes!" and his resumption of his decorous, erect posture informed me that here indeed might be something most interesting. Playing along, I too adopted a prim pose and innocent expression.

Everett returned with, "I'm ducedly sorry, Katherine. It seems a matter has arisen that requires my immediate attention. I fear I must take my leave for the evening."

"Nothing serious, I hope."

"Oh, hardly. A trifling matter of a drunken brawl between two of my junior officers." He sighed, and smiled. "The burden of command, I'm afraid."

James rose as well. "I too should probably be going. I have quite a full day's schedule tomorrow."

After expressing my (more than a little sincere) regret at the ending of the evening's gaiety, I accepted each gentleman's kiss upon my hand as I bid him a good evening.

All the while wondering at just what was in the offing for tomorrow's "adventure" with James.

****

Monday morning found me waiting upon the small wooden wharf at Benbow's Landing at the appointed hour.

The selection of my attire for the day had presented no little problem for Hattie's and my consideration. Though well prepared in my somewhat limited wardrobe for day-to-day affairs, I was altogether lacking in such garb as might be appropriate for "a day upon the river." Indeed, though well versed in matters fashionable, Hattie also was somewhat perplexed as to just what a gentlewoman would wear for such an occupation. Compound our perplexity with the need for me to be sufficiently fetching so as to promote the illusion of innocent, girlish charm, such as to minimize any suspicion should the need arise to facilitate the sharing of confidential information, and the reader can see that more than ordinary attention to vestment was required.

In the end, we settled for a not altogether appropriate, yet not entirely unsuitable, riding habit as my dress for the day. The ensemble consisted of a white linen blouse with generous ruffle at throat and breast, a charcoal-gray skirt over minimal petticoat, a demi-jacket of embroidered gray linen with full "mutton chop" sleeves, and a little hat of black velvet perched at a jaunty angle over my right brow. To emphasize the feminine, I was also provided with a silken parasol in a complimentary shade of dove gray, well endowed with flounce and furbelow, to perch upon my shoulder.

With Hattie in quiet attendance, we had waited for no more than ten minutes before a steam launch of some fifteen or twenty feet of length came *chuff*ing up river, making for the landing upon which I stood. I quickly perceived James attempting (successfully, to my surprise) to cut a dashing figure as he stood in the bows of the little vessel, one foot perched upon the prow, his arms negligently crossed on his upraised thigh. Catching sight of me, he smiled and waved—a wave I returned. His voice carried clearly across the intervening span of water. "Katherine! Oh good! I'm sorry if I'm tardy. We had a bit of trouble firing the boiler."

By now the boat had pulled abreast of the dock. As I smiled and assured him that Hattie and I had been waiting no more than a moment, James, with nimble dexterity, leaped the gap between boat and moorage, and sauntered up to me with an easy, natural grace.

Perhaps I'd been somewhat premature in my appraisal of this fellow. Though no "ancient mariner" as he had intimated aboard the *Elsie Boone*, still his familiarity and comfortable ease in his current situation was readily apparent. James was obviously "at home" upon a river, if not upon the sea.

Taking my proffered hand in his, he gave it a quick brush of his smiling lips. "I'm so glad you could come today. What would have been a day of rote toil, shall now be a fine little adventure, with you to enliven it."

I giggled and endeavored (as usual) to suggest a flush of pleased embarrassment at this compliment. "I'm sure it will be ever so much fun, James. But what *is* the day's activity to be? You've been so mysterious and closed-mouthed about it."

He raised a sardonic eyebrow, and after an oddly familiar echo of another certain seaman's *harrumph*, he groused, "Oh—if I'd said any more of what our day's occupation was to be before that stick-in-the-mud Vincennes, I'm sure he would have forbidden it. But what he does not know, he cannot prohibit, now can he?"

I indicated my assent with a scandalized giggle that was hidden behind an upraised hand. "But surely, you won't get into trouble for this? I don't want to be the cause—"

James snapped his finger and, with a contemptuous little sneer, he said, "Oh, *that* for Vincennes and his trifling—and might I not say, presumptuously rude for their implied lack of trust—regulations. Today we're in my element—the river. Here my judgment holds sway. But come, let's be off."

With that, I was very solicitously assisted onto the launch. I must say that, unaccustomed as I was to boarding small vessels in my masculine guise, it took no skill whatsoever to portray timid femininity as I sought to traverse the gap between pier and boat. The precarious teeter that came at the most dangerous moment as I stood with one foot on the dock, one foot on the rail of the boat, one hand gathering up the volume of my skirts, and one hand grasping my parasol (and therefore, no hands left to regain my balance or grab for assistance) was entirely genuine, containing nothing of premeditation or intentional design.

As he had once before, it was James who came to my rescue.

But this time there was no hesitation in the grasp around my waist, as I was lifted bodily down onto the deck of the boat.

Now I knew there was truth—perhaps more than he suspected—in James' claim that here, upon the river, he was truly within his domain. There was a heretofore absent confidence in his deportment, a surety in his action and his expression that was altogether new.

Interesting.

The better to further my design, in this instance I made no move to distance myself from James, or to give indication that his touch was unwelcome. Indeed, better than I could have devised, my sudden alarm at my precarious situation had raised a flush to my cheeks that could easily be misconstrued as a sudden blush of maidenly ardor. (Success, at last!)

Removing his hands from my waist, with no show this time of fluster or embarrassment, James determined that we were "all aboard," and gave command to cast off from our moorage. (I should mention that during this whole exercise, Hattie, picnic hamper in hand, had been assisted aboard by one of the burly black stokers of the little vessel's boilers.) Turning to me, James indicated a bench in the "stern" (rear) of the boat beneath a canvas awning. "Here, Katherine, sit here in the sheets where you and I can converse as we perform our survey."

Once aboard, and the little vessel now chugging along at steady rate upon the placid river, I found I had no difficulty moving to my seat and claiming it with sufficiently attractive grace and poise. Twirling my parasol on my shoulder and glancing about with genuine interest, I began my investigation. " 'Survey'? What are we examining, James?"

"Ah! Well, in just a moment, you will see."

In fact, it took several minutes for the launch to reach a point, more or less midstream, during which James would give no further hint of our occupation. He only deflected my coaxing questions with a grin and a command to "Wait just a bit more," as he kept eyeing an unremarkable (as far as I could see) spot upon the far shore. Finally, our progress brought us to some apparently salubrious spot, for James abruptly turned to the Negro manning what I believe is called the "helm," and gave orders for "Steerage way only. Hold this spot."

The Negro helmsman's quick reply was a deferential "Yessuh, Cap'n suh," and a quick working of the controls. As the little barque slowed to a stop, James smiled with what I'm sure he thought was secret pleasure at the appellation of "Captain," and turned to a canvas-shrouded device that stood in the center of the after-area of the boat.

Removing the covering, James revealed to me a mechanical device in the form of a circle of metal, of perhaps one foot's diameter, horizontally mounted upon a stubby tripod. Affixed to the top of the circle by a central pivot was a small telescope, from the front of which (nearest the lens) there depended a little spade-shaped weight upon a slender cord. Craning my neck, I could see that the metal circle was engraved about its circumference with finely divided lines, as one might divide the minutes of a clock, and that the little spade-shaped weight was aligned above these markings.

Turning to me and indicating the device, James inquired, "Do you know what this is, Katherine?"

I shook my head in genuine puzzlement.

James continued. "This is called a 'transom'. Land surveyors use it for the measurement of acreage and the like. But I've devised an entirely new usage for it."

As befit Katherine's character, I offered James a polite smile. "Oh, how clever of you!" Then, after a fitting pause, I continued with (genuine) lack of understanding. "Um, what 'usage' might that be?"

In a non-sequitur that would have done Hattie proud, James turned and waved at the breadth of the stream upon which we floated. "How wide would you say the river is at this point?"

I bit my lip in a show of deep concentration, and finally offered an intentionally inaccurate guess: "A mile?"

James chuckled. "No. Though I grant it seems every bit that wide when you're afloat upon it, doesn't it? No. At this point, it is just a little over one hundred yards from shore to shore. Now, you'd think with all that space within which to maneuver, passage up and down such a broad waterway would present no trick at all, wouldn't you?"

I bobbed my head in assent. Then in consternation, I suddenly "changed my mind" and shook my head in the negative, apparently trying to guess the correct answer and thus maintain my standing in my beau's estimation.

James' chuckle became fond indeed. "Well, your latter answer is the correct one. In fact, the broad expanse of the river is deceptive. You see, though the Cooper River is wide, it's very shallow for most of its course until you reach Charleston Harbor, some ten miles downstream from here."

"How shallow?"

"In some cases, no more than two feet. With the exception, that is, of a twisting passage that meanders down the river's length. There, within that passage, the depth is greater: as much as 100 feet in places and never less than 30."

In a reprise of my bluff with Hattie over the matter of ironclad warships, I pretended sagacious comprehension. "Ah, I see."

James continued to smile as he humored my pretended understanding. "Good. Then you can see that a vessel of greater than two feet's draft needs must seek out this deeper channel if it is to safely move up and down the stream? Yes?"

I contrived yet another puzzled frown. " 'Draft'? Do you mean an inconvenient breeze? What's that to do with—"

James' laugh (as I had hoped) was now quite affectionate. (Just such a laugh as you would expect from a man charmed by her naiveté, while attempting to explain a complex idea to a silly—and therefore completely innocent and harmless— little girl.) "No, dearest Katherine. Not a breeze. In this case 'draft' refers to the amount of water a vessel draws. That is to say that the depth to which its keel, its lowest point, extends below the surface of the water."

I nodded, believing that James had made the point sufficiently clear for Katherine's comprehension. James continued. "Now, you might expect this deep channel to proceed more or less down the center of the river, might you not?"

I simply gazed at James in charmed fascination for the marvelously arcane wisdom he was conveying; and made no attempt to indicate, one way or the other, my opinion on this latest proposition.

James was quite content to continue his lecture. "Well, sadly, it does not. Instead, the channel meanders quite willfully; now nearer this shore, now nearer that, now in the center, now twisting about quite unpredictably."

With childlike curiosity I murmured, "But how then does a poor little boat find its way and not bump its—its—"

" 'Keel'?" When I nodded, James folded his arms, his smile now smug indeed. "Well, in years past, that was the job of the river pilot. It was his task to memorize the ever-changing course of the navigable channel and to safely guide vessels under his charge within its bounds."

I frowned in sham consternation. "Safe passage depended on a man's memorization? How daunting! What if his memory failed?"

James' expression became serious for a moment. "Then the vessel might well lose the channel and run aground upon the shallows. And perhaps be damaged or even sunk thereby."

I whimpered a troubled, "Oh, dear!"

James' reply was a solemn nod. "Indeed. But I have devised a way by which the frailties of human memory might be quite removed from the equation."

I again turned that rapt expression on the object of my apparently growing infatuation. "Oh? How?"

In answer, James turned to a small compartment built into the seating of the vessel beside me and, after a moment's consideration, removed a rolled-up document. This he unfurled upon the seat. I beheld a very detailed map of what I perceived to be this section of the river, thickly dotted with arcane symbols, lines, and notations in some indecipherable code.

James directed my attention to this map. "Now then, where on this chart would you say we currently are, Katherine?"

I studied the map for a moment, glanced about the shore for some landmark and then, tentatively, placed my finger on a location that I honestly believed conformed with our present locale.

James nodded and made a little "x" on that place with a pencil. "Good. Your guess makes this interesting for, according to your estimation we're within the bounds of the deep channel. See? Here? This little '28' near where you've pointed? That's a measurement of depth in feet taken as part of a covert survey performed over the last several months. Undertaken, I might mention, by commission from the Navy Department for the sole purpose of enabling my system!"

Next, James turned to his "transom." It was at this point that I noted there was a compass set within the horizontal metal plate, and that the circle itself was mounted on a pivot. This became apparent when James explained, "First, it's necessary to align the azimuth lines with true North." This made no sense to me, but I said nothing as James, very precisely, spun the disk about, all the while examining the compass. At length he was apparently satisfied, for next he peered through the telescopic sight for a moment, evidently searching the far shore for something.

His muttered "Ah, there it is" was indication that he had found what he sought. He motioned me over to the device, and went so far as to offer a steadying touch upon my elbow as I bent and gazed through the eyepiece. "What do you see?"

"I see—Is it the little red square, there, upon the trunk of that tree? The one with the number '8' inscribed upon it?"

James' answered in the affirmative and then again indicated his map. "Now, see?" And he tapped a point on the map. "The notation 'E-8' and the point beside it stand for that target. That's what we call them, those little painted squares: *targets*." James next consulted the metal disk's numbered ring and the little spade-shaped weight. "And Target E-8 bears—117 degrees relative to our position."

I couldn't see what this had to do with anything. "But what—?"

"Patience," James said.

James next withdrew a small, very thin circle of metal, of some four inches in diameter, from a bracket mounted on one of the tripod legs of the transom, together with a metal straight edge approximately one foot in length. I noticed that the little metal circle was also engraved with finely divided numbers about its circumference. Additionally, there was a small hole drilled through its exact center. This hole, James then placed over the little point on the map that corresponded to "E-8". Looking closer, I could see that there were 360 divisions upon the circle, and I quickly deduced (though I did not say) that this corresponded to the 360 degrees of a circle.

Aligning the zero-mark with "North" upon the chart, James then paused for a moment in quick calculation. "Let me see, the complement to 117 is. . .297." He used the straight edge to draw a line across the width of the map's river aligned with the notation corresponding to "297" upon the little disk.

Realizing what was being determined I clapped my hands with glee. "Oh, James, how wonderfully clever! I see now, we're right here." And I laid my finger on the line nearest the little penciled "x" that marked my guess at our location.

I was genuinely surprised (and more than a bit genuinely miffed) when my inspiration was again met by James' gentle laughter. "No, my heart. Think for a moment. You've correctly deduced that a line drawn along an azimuth 297 degrees from a known point relative to us must include our location. But *where* along the *length* of that line is our actual position?"

I frowned, and bit my lip, and realized that I had but guessed when I'd laid my finger on the map. Though I could now hypothesize with more accuracy our actual position, still—

I turned my frustrated (and fetching?) gaze on James. His reply was a reprise of that knowing smirk, and a little sidelong nod toward the opposite shore from that we had just been studying.

I believed I understood what was being hinted at, but I feigned continuing perplexity as befit Katherine's scatter-brained character.

The perplexity became genuine when I failed to espy any red squares on the opposite shore. I was about to make my confusion known to James when my eyes came to rest not on a red square, but a green one. This I quickly pointed to, eliciting a brisk nod and a congratulatory smile from James.

More sightings were taken, now upon the green square. Another line was drawn, more or less perpendicular to the first line. James then tapped the intersection of the two lines. "Do you see? Where these lines meet, there is our actual position."

I did finally understand, and I admit my next exclamation of, "Oh, how magical!" was more authentic that artifice.

James graciously accepted my praise, then again indicated the chart. "Now, see here? See where our actual position is in relation to your initial guess?" I examined the chart. The distance didn't seem that far off to me; and with a little sniff of pride and a smug expression, I made that point.

James folded his arms and grinned in triumph. "Indeed, Katherine. The distance between guess and reality is not that great. No more than a few dozen yards. But look—the depth here is—"

And we both examined the map. With chastened voice, I mumbled, "Oh—'four feet'."

"Indeed. And well out of the safe channel. A vessel drawing more than four feet would run aground here."

"Oh, dear," I said. But I was not truly feeling distressed; quite the contrary. In a flash of inspiration, the plot by which I might dash all of the Confederacy's hopes in this endeavor suddenly revealed itself to me.

It took all the thespian skill I could muster to feign mild interest in the next question: "How is the location of the 'targets' determined? By what calculation?"

James gave a little shake of his head. "There is no particular science to their placement. The only requisite is that they be readily visible from a vessel and at such interval as to cover an appropriate stretch of water."

I continued in thoughtful tones. "But surely, there is little margin for error in the calculations. Isn't there some requirement—?"

"Indeed. There is perishingly small margin for error. When the distance from target to vessel is great, even a mistake of a few degrees can have profound effect." James proceeded to demonstrate this by recalculating and redrawing his two lines, in each case intentionally misaligning them by two degrees. The resulting erroneous report of our position, I was secretly intrigued to note, placed us a goodly number of yards away from our actual locale.

My tones were now thoughtful indeed.

"How interesting—"

James spoke in an animated tone. "Ah, but you haven't seen the best yet! Look again at the map." I obeyed and he continued. "Consider how the method might be expanded upon. We know we are here." He tapped the map at the original intersection of lines. "As you can see the safe channel extends hence at a bearing of"—more resort to his little metal disk—"192 degrees for a distance of"—employment of the calibrated straight edge—"a distance of 241 yards." He made another little "x" at the point where the channel suddenly veered away to the left. "At that point, targets E-9 and W-9 bear"—more recourse to the small disk, taking the newly-marked "x" as its alignment point upon the map—"87 and 202 degrees respectively."

I considered the truth of this with bitten lip and hands absent-mindedly smoothing the front of my blouse as I pondered the riddle. "Um, yes. It's all quite magical, and ever so clever. But, um—"

He cocked his head on his shoulder, his expression once again a fond grin. "But what has that to do with anything? How is that important?"

I turned to him, winsome incomprehension writ large on my features.

He folded his arms, the smile now perhaps a bit smug as well. "Using the method I've just demonstrated, you can see how a vessel might chart a safe passage in advance of its actual voyage and could therefore proceed at a relatively quick pace. Quite the improvement over a stumbling, groping advance based on frail human memory and lead-line readings of depth taken every few hundred yards."

I could see how this would be so, and the boon it presented to riverine navigation and commerce, and said as much.

Still James was not finished, and now came the most intriguing revelation of all. "There is one final advantage my method confers." He rolled up the map he'd been using, and withdrew a new chart from the cabinet, which he unfolded. "Now, see here, Katherine? This is the chart of Charleston Harbor. Again, you can see how targets have been affixed at various locales around the shoreline. Further, you can see by the depth notations that the harbor itself has its many reefs and shoals, depths and shallows, all of which have been carefully charted."

Nodding, I hypothesized, "So, by your method, it would be possible to navigate about in the harbor with as much ease as up and down the river."

With sudden vehemence, James declared, "Yes! And that, perhaps even more than her armor or her weapons, will be *Moultrie*'s decisive advantage."

"I'm sorry, dear James. For a moment I thought I comprehended, but—"

James reined in his enthusiasm, returning to that pedantic tone. "Oh, your pardon. Of course it must seem mysterious to you because you don't yet know what *Moultrie*'s purpose is."

Anticipating that I was about to garner a crucial tidbit, I continued to portray fawning fascination, though my very genuine eagerness for James to make his revelation was taxing my acting skills to the limit.

"And what, kind sir, might that purpose be?"

James glanced sidelong at me, feminine and fetching and apparently so close to being won over by his prowess and importance. The temptation was apparently too great, for in a quietly confidential tone, he said, "Why, the breaking of the blockade of Charleston Harbor, of course."

My eyes went wide with surprise, to which I quickly added (feigned) admiration, just as I'm sure James had wished. "Oh, James! Truly? Oh, how marvelous! What a blow that will be to those Yankee villains!"

He nodded and continued in that confidential tone: "Perhaps more than you know, Katherine. It's rumored that several European powers are seriously considering recognition of the Confederacy. If we were to receive such desperately needed validation, and the financial and material support that would attend, the prospect for a successful conclusion of this conflict would be greatly enhanced. Such a decisive victory as the shattering of the Charleston Blockade, as symbolic as that victory would be, might be just the motivation those Europeans need to finally sway their decision in our favor."

"Oh, James—how positively thrilling! When is all of this to take place? How soon?"

"By all estimation, *Moultrie* will be combat-worthy within two weeks. And once she is loosed upon the Yankee rascals, think of the advantage my method will provide her as she glides about with nimble grace, always assured of sufficient depth beneath her keel while her adversaries stumble and fumble with no foreknowledge whatsoever as to what is beneath them or in which direction they may safely maneuver. And all the while, *Moultrie*'s impenetrable armor protects her from harm, as her own formidable batteries rain down destruction upon her confused foes."

I clapped my hands with false glee. "Delightful! Oh, how brave and beautiful she will be! And how disconcerted will be her adversaries! And to think, I'm to be here to witness it all take place! Perhaps, with our efforts today, I might even be allowed some small mention in the final outcome!"

He gave me an indulgent little smile. "Oh, yes. I'm sure that may well be the case."

I said truthfully, "I hope so."

I felt overjoyed at that moment. I felt everything was going my way.

To which, Dame Fortune pointed at me and cackled.

XII.
The Plot Attempted

But that same day as my river outing—only a few hours later, in fact—Digny came riding in haste up to my front door. With great disquiet, he thrust himself into my presence as I was taking breakfast in the grand salon.

Barging in without so much as a polite knock or civil announcement, he accosted me with, "Na—Katherine. Disturbing news!"

Glaring at him, I dismissed the servants who attended me, all but Hattie whom I commanded to close the doors after their departure. When we were alone, I chided Digny, "Honestly, sir! Calm yourself before you give us all away through some foolish slip of the tongue!"

"But discovery is the very theme of my dreadful news!"

A cold, leaden weight settled in the pit of my stomach. " 'Discovery,' you say? By whom? How?"

He reached into his ever-present portmanteau and withdrew a letter. Even before I could peruse it, he was whimpering, "It is from Katherine—*the real Katherine Bonveneau!* It seems that her proposed wedding has been called off, her engagement annulled! She instructs me to suspend my attempts to sell Belle Bois as *she intends to return within two weeks and reclaim possession!* What shall we do? We are discovered!"

I considered the implication of this, and with distracted tones commanded, "Mr. Digny, really. Calm yourself. If we had been discovered, we would not be chatting so amiably here in my dining room. We'd be in the depths of the Charleston City jail awaiting our fate."

This sent Digny into fresh, but thankfully quiet, paroxysms. Hattie, from her station beside the barred doors, observed, "Still, this is grave indeed, Nathan. It seems that this particular impersonation has come to an end, and that our best course would be to abandon it and flee at the first opportunity."

"Perhaps. But duce it, Hattie—the opportunity we have here is so tantalizing that I am loath to miss it. A successful voyage by *Moultrie* is so fraught with peril for the Union's cause—There must be some way—"

Hattie growled, "Not unless you can devise some method to prevent the inevitable return of the genuine Katherine and the discovery that would precipitate. And I can see no way to avoid that if we remain here."

And then, seated there, in another flash of sudden clarity, I beheld the second facet of my grand design. With the beginnings of a smile, I turned to my two compatriots and whispered, "No. Not avoid discovery—*invite it!*"

They exchanged a glance that proclaimed their sudden fear for my sanity. I only forged ahead. "Mr. Digny. I need you to convey an urgent and complex message to Niles and Captain Wickman. Can this be done with speed? Time is perilously short, or I miss my guess."

"I—if the need is urgent, it might be done—"

"Good. Take down this message."

As I dictated my intent, the white lawyer and the black woman shared worried looks.

In truth, I was worried, too—at least as much as Hattie. But to have even a small chance of success with my mad scheme, I had to convince Hattie and Digny that I was the apex of confidence.

****

And so, the days for the fulfillment of my first mission on behalf of the Union were finally accomplished, and the time for decisive action at last arrived.

Hattie and I determined that the best time for the implementation of our stroke against the *Moultrie* would probably be in the hours of darkness just before her sally against the Union fleet.

But we came to this conclusion only after fierce debate.

The timing of the sabotage was first raised in what had become our "War Room"—the cloister of my boudoir—on the evening of my sojourn upon the river with James.

I was all for attempting the sabotage that I intended, that very night, as soon as full darkness had descended.

Hattie, in essence, called me an idiot: "Going tonight would be unwise, Nathan. I think it prudent that we delay, waiting until the last possible moment before *Moultrie*'s sailing."

"*What?* Have you taken leave of your senses?"

This was the first time I ever saw Hattie's normally placid features scowl. " 'Leave of my senses' how?"

I tried to moderate my tone, though how the normally insightful Hattie could fail to perceive the threat that any delay would bring, was puzzling to me. "Have you forgotten about the impending doom of genuine-Katherine's arrival? Who knows what span of time remains to us—if any time remains at all!"

But Hattie only shook her head. "There is a far greater threat to the scheme that trumps that fear."

"*What?* What possible threat could trump the fear of exposure, and what that exposure would entail?"

"Nathan, please—stop and consider. Yes, the genuine Katherine's arrival would indeed be ruinous, in that it would force us to abandon the current scheme. But just as perilous would be the premature discovery of the scheme's existence!"

" 'Premature discovery'? What am I to make of that? 'Discovery' how?"

Now Hattie's scowl deepened. "Did you not just spend the whole afternoon upon the river with Eddiborogh, as he inspected and calibrated his devices?"

"What has that to do with—"

"What would be the outcome if, after what you intend, Eddiborogh were to engage in subsequent inspection?"

"He would not do so; he would have no reason to."

Hattie shrugged. "Still, what if he *did* inspect the targets again? He would have the time."

At last I saw what Hattie had seen. I whispered, "The sabotage would be found." *And "Katherine" would become an immediate suspect therefrom.*

Bless Hattie. Seeing that her point had been made, she undertook no attempt to press it further at my expense.

And yet, for vanity if nothing else, I couldn't help but attempt one last defense of my desire for immediate action. "But if we delay and Katherine—the genuine Katherine, that is—were to arrive—"

Hattie merely shrugged. "Then the scheme would come to nothing anyway, no matter when it was attempted—now or later—because any enterprise that the bogus Katherine had tainted would be scrutinized."

In the end, I could find no flaw in Hattie's reasoning and thus, though it surely chafed every waking moment of the interval between idea and implementation, Hattie's counsel prevailed.

So we waited.

****

But at last, the fateful night arrived.

At a little after midnight, Hattie and I silently moved through our sleeping household toward the kitchen door. It seemed that the risk of discovery was sufficiently small, and outweighed any benefit to be gained by again resorting to our disused shed staging area, and so I went forth in masculine guise.

Given some of the examples that had gone before, my chosen character for this phase of our endeavor was in comparison quite ordinary. A simple suit of workaday clothes, such as might be worn by a young tradesman, and my undisguised male visage comprised the whole of this character. It was Hattie's and my belief that, were I detained in this guise, there would be nothing amiss to discover, should a detailed examination of my person result. As to challenges of my identity or my business—well, we would simply have to trust to Providence and my quick wit to provide.

Opening the door as quietly as possible, Hattie surprised me with a quick embrace and a whispered farewell of "Be safe, Nathan. Return soon." (As the presence of a Negro out and about at night was difficult to explain under the best of circumstances, Hattie reluctantly had agreed that this outing was one I must undertake alone.)

The night was dark, but not deeply so. A "hunter's moon" rode high in the heavens, shedding such light as made a lantern unnecessary.

It's strange to relate but, at least at first, my activities proceed quite without alarum or challenge. I had expected the navigational targets to be defended somehow. Of course, absent my own nefarious intent, who would have anticipated the need to secure them?

In the event, the only source of anxiety for me was the unavoidable noise produced when I employed a pry bar to remove the target from whatever tree it had been affixed to, and then the even greater noise produced by the (muffled as it was with a scrap of canvas wrapped about its head) hammer I used to nail the target back upon some different tree, a bit removed in one direction or another from its original site.

I had made substantial progress, having altered the position of fully six of the targets, when, as I was endeavoring to alter the seventh, it occurred to me that I had erred, perhaps grievously. The tree of Target Seven's original installation was a sizeable old oak, once apparently split by lightning, and therefore very unique for its twisted and bizarre shape. I had given no thought to the fact that, if moved from such a memorable spot in favor of a wholly unremarkable new tree, the alteration might be noticed and the sabotage revealed thereby.

With a mental curse, I quickly replaced Target Seven in as close to its original situation as I could devise. Then, realizing that I had made a similar faux pas in altering Target Three, (from the wall of a riverside shed to fairly distant tree,) I determined that my best course might be to call a halt to any further alterations, (trusting to Fate that the amount of mischief already done was sufficient for my cause,) and to retrace my route, returning Target Three to its original location before retiring back to Belle Bois.

Again, my good fortune held as I wended my way back along my route. I was not, to my knowledge, observed and certainly was not challenged. Indeed, all proceeded well up to the point when I had finished hammering in the nails that held Target Three to the wall of its shed.

It was as I was standing there in the gloom, admiring my handiwork, when, I don't know by what means (perhaps by some little telltale sound that operated more upon my subconscious than my perception), I became aware that someone was approaching.

Glancing about, I realized that there was no good place of concealment for several dozen yards in any direction. If I were to flee, it was almost assured that I would be noticed, and that by that action, (being observed while dashing for cover,) the hue and cry would fairly be raised. In desperation, I ducked inside the shed, drawing the door partly closed behind me and then pressing an anxious eye to the crack.

Almost immediately I observed two individuals, one tall and armed with a pitchfork, one elderly and provided with what I took to be a shotgun, emerge from the woods a little to the left of my place of concealment. The elderly fellow glanced about, and I heard him mutter, "I'm sure I heard a noise from over here."

The taller, pitchfork-wielding fellow grunted, "I di'n't hear nothin', Pa."

"You hush, now, Ike. And look sharp. There's deviltry afoot. I can feel it."

"Don't see nobody, Pa."

But "Pa" was now regarding the shed with what (in the now seemingly dazzling shine of the moon) I could tell was a suspicious frown.

"Here now. I wonder—that shed—"

Discovery was at hand. It must have been sheer panic and desperation that supplied me with my next course.

As Pa and Ike approached the shed, alert for any sudden surprise, they were nevertheless quite amazed to hear issuing from within, a feminine moan of passion followed by a breathlessly eager woman's voice crying, "Oh, Silas—your lips—they're like fire! Oh, my darling! Take me in your arms and kiss me again!"

It was Ike who in rather a loud voice exclaimed, "What the devil is goin' on here?"

This produced a sudden stillness from within the shed, followed by the frantic rustle of cloth and a now-panicked feminine whimper of, "Oh, god! We're found! What will we do? If Father discovers—"

This was quickly answered by a rather gruff masculine voice, which in worried tones, replied, "Hush, my sweet. Stay here, stay quiet. I'll see what transpires."

****

The door to the shed slowly opens, and a pale, anxious young man's face peers out into the night.

Pa speaks, "You there. Come out so's we can see you!"

The male at the shed's door attempts to bluster his way past the difficulty: "See here! Who are you, and what's your business?"

The older man's tone becomes more officious. "Never you mind who I am. All you needs to know is that it's the Hanahan Township Citizen's Vigilance Committee that orders you to come outta there."

The male face disappears for a moment; from within, a now tearful woman's voice sobs, "Oh, my love! We're undone!"

Silas replies, (his shaky voice quite failing to convey the confidence he is trying to feign for his lady's reassurance,) "Perhaps all is not lost. Remain hidden, and I'll try to reason with them."

And with that, the young man steps hesitantly out into the open.

He is greeted by a knowing frown (from Pa) and a salacious leer (from Ike). Again Pa speaks: "So, boy. What was you doin' in there, hey?"

"Silas" casts about with guilty expression. "Why, nothing. Nothing at all."

Ike giggles, "Din't soun' lik' nothin' ta me! Sounded like a whole heap o' somethin'!"

Pa growls, "Shut up, you."

Then Pa turns again to Silas. "You ain't foolin' nobody, son. Now, you fetch that missy outta there, and we're gonna straighten this out!"

Silas panics: "Oh, no! Oh, sir, I beg you! Please—The young lady—if her identity becomes known, her father—For pity's sake, gentlemen, spare us! All would be ruined!"

"Ruined? Maybe it should be! Carryin' on in the middle o' the night in some back barn! Shame on you! Shame on the both o' you!"

Silas stares at the ground at his feet. "I swear to you, all is not as it appears. My intentions toward—toward the young lady are most honorable. But you see—her father forbids us. And not for any good cause! He has made it plain that his daughter will never marry, unless it is to such wealth that he may retire to idleness and luxury on the coattails of his new son-in-law. So because of our deep love for one another, Abi—the young woman—and I have carried on such liaison as we could contrive, always in secret. Always undiscovered— until now. And just as it has befallen that within the week, I am to receive a sizable inheritance from my uncle who has fallen in battle. As soon as the bequest is officially announced, all bar to our open declaration of our intention to wed will be removed."

Pa says, "But boy—"

"Oh, sirs, I know it was wrong of us to continue to meet in secret. But the joy of the upcoming time when we might finally be together—Oh, please, can you not understand? Both our forgivable eagerness and how discovery of our forbidden liaison now would surely ruin all? For charity and in the name of love, can you not, but this once, overlook your discovery?"

Pa strokes a bristled chin and considers. "Hmm—well. I'll do this for you. What's your name, boy?"

The young lad squares his shoulders, and in a firm voice proclaims, "Silas Wickman, sir."

"Very well, young Silas Wickman. I remember what it is to love a woman, and what it can drive a man to. And while I don't hold with such skulkin' about, I can see how it were at least partly the fault of your lady's pap's idleness and greed. So—I'll give you a week. But you mark me, now. I'll have an eye out down to the County Recorder's Office. If, by the end o' that week, I doesn't see banns o' matrimony proposed for one

Silas Wickman to wed some young lass o' this county, why then that Mr. Wickman is gonna have the Devil to pay. You believe it!"

With overwhelming relief, young Silas nods and smiles. "Oh yes, sir! It shall be as you say! One week—yes! That can be accomplished, I swear to it!"

The old man offers a grudging smile in return. "See to it you do! Now, Ike an' me is gonna mosey off down that away." He nods toward the south. "We'll be back this way directly. I'd say once we was gone, why that'd be a good chance for a gentleman to get a proper young lady back safe behind her doors, without any further discovery by the night watch. If you takes my meanin'."

Again Silas nods. "Oh, yes! To be sure, I do!"

Without further comment, Pa and a still grinning Ike make their way back into the underbrush and so disappear.

****

Breathing a silent prayer of thanksgiving, I followed Pa's advice, and made all haste to get a certain "proper young lady" back safe behind her doors.

****

What transpired on the following day shall live forever indelibly etched upon my memory.

XIII.
Consequences

It was the morning after I had moved the targets.

As might be guessed, by this time, and despite Everett's best efforts to prevent it, word of the coming voyage of the *Moultrie* had become something of an "open secret." Though it might well be thought that, but for the persons directly engaged in one way or another with the project, out of all of the other residents of the community, mine was the most complete understanding of what was actually to transpire.

Nevertheless, the morning after my nocturnal escapade found the countryside quite abuzz with speculation and rumors that something very noteworthy would transpire upon the river this day. Indeed, when at the urging of my now overwhelming need to observe the result of my handiwork of the previous night, once suitably disguised as Katherine, I adjourned to that same Benbow's Landing where James and I had embarked on the day of our "survey."

I found that place already populated with several dozen members of the local gentry, desporting themselves as though they were attending upon some out-of-doors festivity or picnic.

It was as I was exchanging greetings and inconsequential pleasantries with diverse members of the crowd that a cry of "There, coming around the bend. What is that?" turned all eyes in the direction indicated.

Proceeding at a goodly pace beneath a towering cloud of black coal smoke that was laced with feathers of steam, I now had my first glimpse of the enemy object of all of my efforts: *C.S.S. Moultrie.*

I confess that at first, I wasn't quite sure what it was that I beheld. To date, my only contact with naval vessels had been of the then-conventional design—to wit, a sturdy hull populated with one or more tall masts; and perhaps, in the more modern designs, a smokestack and paddle wheels (either at the back or in the middle). But here, sailing briskly in my direction, was a creature most strange.

In form, *Moultrie* might best be described as a tent-shaped affair of some fifty or sixty feet of length and perhaps twenty of width, the sides of the tent being composed of metal plate painted a glossy black. At each end of this elongated pyramid, (fore and aft) there were two cylindrical—well, for all the world I was reminded of the turrets of an ancient castle, though these were again formed of that same black metal, and possessed of a window-like slit that proceeded around their circumference. From these two embrasures, there protruded the muzzles of a pair of most formidable-looking field pieces, one weapon to each "turret." The whole contrivance was topped by a small, armored wheelhouse located a bit forward of her center, and a large smokestack located a bit behind.

But of this entire exotic engine, it was the suddenly noticed flag she flew that elicited the greatest attention of the onlookers. Flying from a pole erected atop the wheelhouse, snapping smartly in the wind of *Moultrie*'s passage, was the battle ensign of the Confederacy.

Amid cheers from others, a male voice near me said loudly, "Y'all, two hours from now, those Yankees in Charleston Harbor will all be dead or run away like whipped dogs, you mark my words."

The lusty cheer that went up from the small crowd there upon the jetty must have been quite heartening to the sailors aboard that vessel. I must say, even I felt a smile of enthusiasm for the moment grace my lips.

That smile was short-lived.

By some design of Fate, the poor, doomed vessel had almost drawn abreast of my location when one of the men standing in the small crowd remarked, "Here, now! She's awfully far to the east of the channel. I wonder what—"

There was a deep vibration, more felt through our feet than heard. Smiles of hope and encouragement turned to frowns of puzzlement.

Another vibration. Then another. *Moultrie* began to slew sharply to the left of her original track, and the water about her hull began to roil with mud. The same individual who had just spoken, moaned, "Oh God, she's run aground!"

But that was not all.

Suddenly the smokestack belched a huge plume of white steam in place of the black smoke that had been pouring forth. Then followed a deep, and this time very audible, rumbling report, followed by an eldritch shriek—as though some tortured soul trapped within the metal leviathan cried out for salvation.

A middle-aged woman whimpered, "John, what's that noise? What's happening?"

A heartsick male voice replied, "She must have breached her hull. When the cold water touches the hot metal of the boilers, the stress is too great and they explode! Oh Lord, the poor men—"

Little doors were flung wide, and the desperate sailors were seen to be flinging themselves into the river to escape the sudden explosive rush of steam from demolished boilers that signaled the doom of their vessel.

I remember, above all the noise and tumult, the soft weeping of some woman standing to my left, as she watched this valiant hope of her young nation dying before her eyes. I remember a little voice of reason, speaking in my mind, urging me to counterfeit some similar show of emotion as might befit the feminine character I portrayed.

But through it all, I could only stand there, my arms hanging lifelessly at my sides, my jaw slack and amazed as I watched the deviltry that I had ordained, unfold before me.

By noon, all had been accomplished. Poor, valiant *Moultrie*'s entire career was to be a voyage of a little under eight miles.

****

In subsequent months there were some proposals to attempt repair. But in the end, the scarcity of resources, so desperately needed in other theaters of the war, made any thoughts of resurrecting the hulk untenable. She was stripped of her metal armor, and such valuable tackle and what equipment could be salvaged. Her oaken skeleton remained for a few months before even it was scavenged, a silent monument to the failure of one of the South's greatest and now forgotten hopes.

Monument also to the ruination of a young man's career.

Though the sabotage of the navigational aids was ultimately discovered, the damage had been done. Though James Eddiborogh was absolved of any incompetence, that absolution came at the behest of a Confederate Board of Inquiry. With the ending of the War, the victorious Northern authorities could be little bothered with such triviality as to recognize the exoneration of one Southern river pilot who might have potentially played so large a role in what could have been, for the Northern forces, such a devastating defeat.

James Eddiborogh died of pneumonia in the winter of 1867, there in the squalid Washington hotel room to which he had been reduced as he desperately pursued the impossible dream of petitioning uncaring Department of the Navy bureaucrats. He died still seeking the unattainable goal of clearing his reputation, of saving himself from the fate he ultimately suffered: the anonymous death of a dishonored, forgotten man.

I wonder if it brings him comfort when he considers the subsequent pains that Hattie and I, the architects of his destruction, suffered?

XIV.
Alarums and Excursions

I set the following down in the most objective fashion I can contrive, that the reader may have the clearest understanding of the events that I relate.

The day of Hattie's and my great "undoing," coming but five days following the demise of the *Moultrie*, was ordinary enough until a little after four in the afternoon. As was her custom, Katherine had just risen from her afternoon "withdrawal," when there was a commotion out in the lane.

That same stylishly appointed brougham as I had seen before, and four stalwarts of the local mounted militia, clattered up before the front door. The militiamen dismounted. From the carriage stepped Major Vincennes, a deeply pensive expression clouding his already so-tragic countenance.

At his knock, young Adam admitted him, and then scampered before him to try and rouse either Old Tub or perhaps to find Hattie. He had not ventured far, with the Major close upon his heels, when the lady of the household, Katherine herself, accosted the Major from the head of the grand staircase.

"Everett? What an unexpected pleasure. I was just—"

But the Major held aloft his hand and silenced her thought. "Madam, excuse me but—Forgive this rude intrusion on your afternoon's routine. I must tell you that I am here today in my official capacity as the Commander of Militia."

Her brow clouds at his officious tone. " 'As the commander of the militia'? Whatever for? Everett, what are those armed men doing on my porch? What is all this fuss about?"

But his tone remains cold and very officious. "Those men are here at my command. There has been disturbing news from Richmond. Perhaps you had best come down and we'll adjourn to your parlor. This needs discussion."

She descends the stairs in a swirl of crinoline, her body servant Hattie close behind, a look of quiet concern to match that of her mistress upon Hattie's dusky brow. Finally standing before her guest, Katherine tries to read meaning in her cavalier's eyes. "Everett, what is this all about? What news have you received?"

The Major, for the first time, looks a bit nonplussed. Perhaps it is Katherine's nearness that is beginning to unman him. "Madam, please. Perhaps if we could adjourn—?"

" 'Madam'? Everett, you're beginning to frighten me. It is I, Katherine. Since you rescued me at the railroad station, when has 'Madam' been necessary between us?"

The Major is beginning to frame a reply when there is renewed commotion out in the lane.

A new carriage has arrived, escorted by a pair of mounted men in regular uniform. From it alights a tall fellow, fiercely bearded and mustachioed, dressed in the uniform of a colonel of cavalry. Behind him, a small, feminine figure waits to be assisted from her conveyance.

This new pair then proceeds, the small woman setting a brisk pace, toward the grand entranceway. The doors are opened by the guarding militiamen.

In an instant, the small, blonde figure stands hands upon her hips, glaring at the tableau of Major, Katherine, and Hattie. For his part, the Major stares, agog, at the face of this female newcomer.

A face that looks like Katherine's face, but under blond hair.

At seeing this same face, a small moan of despair escapes Hattie's lips.

The blonde stares daggers at the Negress, and nods once in confirmation of some suspicion. "So! You're here too, are you? How wonderful! Traitorous wretch! Now you'll get your due!"

Katherine tries to match her female guest's obvious fury with bluster of her own: "See here! Who are you? How dare you come barging into my home—"

The Blonde Fury swings on Katherine. " 'Your' home? *'Your' home?* Shall we speak of gall? How dare you confront me in *my* foyer with such bald effrontery, and demand to know my business?"

Katherine now tries to appeal to the Major. "Who is this madwoman?"

The little blonde makes to spring forward, but the cavalry Colonel restrains her.

Finally she splutters, "Who am I, indeed! You thief! You unspeakable *usurper!* I am *Katherine Bonveneau, the woman whose name and life you have so shamelessly attempted to steal!* And for that outrage, reckoning is now at hand! Colonel, perform your office! Arrest that imposter!"

And a finger, trembling with barely suppressed rage, stabs at Katherine.

Katherine stares wildly from face to face, all of the color quite drained from her cheeks. "I—there's been some mistake, surely—Everett?"

The small blonde turns to the Major with a glare. " 'Everett'? Everett Vincennes? How you've grown from the boy I remember."

Everett's charming smile dies a stillbirth as she continues. "The arrogant bully who, purely for spite and the admiration of his ragtag band of juvenile admirers, once pushed a helpless little girl several years his junior into a mud puddle, thus ruining my favorite dress. Oh, yes, I remember you! And by the flame on your cheeks, I see you remember me as well!"

Everett lapses into a mortified silence.

The Colonel now steps forward. In a well-bred South Carolina drawl, the colonel declares, "There are other matters to be answered for as well. Matters that have caused me to be dispatched from Governor Ainsworth's office with instructions to take the woman purporting to be Katherine Bonveneau into custody, and transport her back to Richmond that she may attempt to answer them."

The Major spares a glance at this gentleman. "And you, sir, are—?"

"Colonel Faircloth, at your service, sir. Here are my warrants and assurance of my identity." The Colonel passes several folded papers to the Major, which he briefly examines. Finally the Major nods, and hands the papers back.

Turning on the trembling brunette, Major Vincennes nods toward the waiting escort. "Madam—and now I use that term with more assurance than before, for now I truly hesitate to call you *Katherine*. You will accompany this officer, as his warrants seem well in order."

"Everett, please—"

"No! So much now becomes clear to me. A certain strange occurrence at the Goose Creek Yard's checkpoint. Your often 'unreliable' memory of such events from your past as might be expected to be much more clear in your mind. Your dalliance with Eddiborogh, and his mysterious incompetence leading to the grounding of the *Moultrie*. No, madam, no! Too many coincidences now pile one atop the other. If I am mistaken in my suspicions, you shall have my most abject apology. But I begin to suspect that such apology will not be soon forthcoming."

Throughout all this confrontation, Hattie has been slowly backing away, apparently seeking refuge or perhaps escape.

Now the little blonde—the newly proclaimed genuine Katherine, Mistress of Belle Bois—stabs that accusatory finger at the retreating servant. "Seize her! If there was further proof required, you need only look in that perfidious wench's face to see it! She knows me, don't you, you despicable cur? Just as I know you. Hattie—worthless whelp of that equally worthless Maddie, my once Nurse who absconded all those years ago, abandoning me to my subsequent banishment and—and—"

She struggles to finish the thought, but the words catch in her throat with the magnitude of her rage and pain.

Hattie now raises her hands in supplication. "Mist'us Kate, please—mercy! I was but a child myself then, and not responsible. Now I only undertook what I was ordered—"

This time the little blonde won't be restrained. Springing forward, she slaps the cowering unfortunate hard enough to turn her head. *"SILENCE! No more of your lies!* You will never open your mouth again, but with my permission! *Do you hear me? Do you?"*

Turning to the now-gathered servants, the true Katherine espies the one white face in the throng and demands, "You— are you the overseer?"

Jeb Hawlsey, but newly arrived at the scene of this confusion, looks uncertainly from face to face. "I am."

Katherine thrusts the quaking Hattie in his direction. "Then take this mutinous trash out back and flog her! Do you understand?"

Her rage has risen to the point where she appears on the verge of apoplexy. Her full skirts swirl with the stamp of her foot that is caused by the lack of instantaneous obedience to her command.

"TAKE THIS NIGGER OUT AND FLOG HER! NOW!"

Jeb's confusion only grows. He tries to catch the eye of the imposter Katherine, but she only stares at the ground, pinioned in the grasp of the Colonel who has moved forward to apprehend her.

It is only when Major Vincennes, the one person Jeb knows to be in authority, nods and repeats Katherine's command, that the now-nerveless Hattie is led away to the pillory out near the slave quarters.

Jeb fellows close behind Hattie, his expression becoming a brutal grin at the prospect of the task at hand.

The blonde Katherine, herself showing a smug grin, rounds on the imposter. "So. Your evil schemes have finally come home to roost, have they? What have you to say now? No further protestations of innocence? No more attempts to abscond with my virtue and my good name?"

The Imposter can only shake her head, and meekly allow herself to be led away.

The Major offers to detail a troop of his cavalry to add to the Colonel's escort, but the Colonel's quiet assurance that he and his men can easily deal with any offer of resistance on the part of this petite woman is sufficient for the Major.

Once the Colonel and his charge have ascended into the Colonel's carriage, and they and their escort have departed, the Major makes an abortive attempt to take some kind of civil leave from the newly installed mistress of the household.

But she will have none of it: "Major Vincennes, it is manifestly clear that either through criminal incompetence or actual complicity, you are as much to blame for the current state of affairs as anyone. It should be unnecessary therefore, for me to ask a purported gentleman to kindly remove himself from my premises immediately, and to do me the courtesy not to trouble me further. Ever! Good day, sir!"

With that, the door slams in his face, bringing the afternoon's festivities to an abrupt conclusion.

****

My chance did not come until well past nine o'clock that evening, when the occupants of Belle Bois had retired.

With great care and caution, my skirts gathered firmly into my grasp so as to silence my progress, I made my way to the small outbuilding. Not until I was within, and the door bolted behind me, did I strike a lucifer and set flame to the small stub of candle I had smuggled there.

Even in the candle's glow, it was a moment before I saw Hattie.

I can truly say: Not until that instant, had I ever really understood. But seeing her, laying there upon the coarse, filthy straw—I have no words to convey the crippling shame for my past uncaring, unfeeling sentiments, and the heart-wrenching sorrow I now felt for man's capacity to injure his fellow.

I think, perhaps, she had been drowsing, for it was not until I had been standing there for a moment, steeped in my shame and sorrow, that Hattie stirred and opened her eyes. Those deep pools that had looked more than once into my soul with tolerance for my many foolish errors, now brightened at my approach. In that instant, truly, my heart broke. For even now, at this juncture, I still read understanding and forgiveness there.

Her voice was a strong though quiet murmur: "Ah, Nathan, there you are. I haven't yet had the opportunity to tell you that I approve of you as a blonde. That color much suits your eyes."

"Hattie—"

Her lips curled into a gentle smile. How could this be? How could she even deign to acknowledge me while she lay there, huddled in the simple, wretched clothing, within which she had willingly debased herself to play the role of slave? Clothing now rent from waist to shoulders—shoulders raw and torn from the lash. How could it be that in this most abused state, still she could smile with such warmth at the author of her agony?

"Hattie—Oh, god—"

"Shh, Nathan. It is a little thing and I have survived it."

" 'A little thing'? How can you say this? How can you even bear to have me near you? Oh, Hattie, forgive me."

"Forgive? What would you have me forgive? All transpired as we ordered it. Never forget, dearest Nathan, this—"

She stirred a bit, and for the first and last time, a sharp intake of breath escaped her lips, as testament to the agony she still no doubt suffered.

"—this was every bit as much my own invention as yours. Less than this, and doubts might have lingered in too many minds. She that could be impersonated once, might she not be impersonated again? But now I dare say that all doubts as to the authenticity of this latest iteration of Katherine Bonveneau have been laid to rest. Who but the genuine mistress would be so bold as to order the flogging of one of her slaves? And what slave would deign to suffer that fate, unless it was ordered by anyone but her true mistress?"

I knelt beside her. "No *slave* would suffer it, Hattie. Only a woman of such courageous strength and will that she would—"

But my words, so small and trivial, caught in my throat, and I could only lower my head in my ever-deepening shame.

Hattie's gentle touch upon my cheek was absolution.

"It is past, Nathan. It is over, and we are the stronger for it. Now ease my mind."

As a drowning man clutches a line, I pressed Hattie's hand to my cheek. "How? Tell me how I may, Hattie, and what is in my power—"

"Your sister, Elizabeth—Is she safe? Out of harm's way?"

I nodded. "Yes. Word came from Niles not an hour ago. He reported that they were all safely away down the river. By now they have reached the blockade fleet out in Charleston Bay, and are out of peril."

"You must compliment her for me, Nathan. I do believe acting must run in your family, for her double impersonation of you playing Katherine was quite masterful. I don't doubt but that everyone who saw it was quite as taken-in as the good Major."

I found a smile to offer this remarkable woman. "Here, now! I'll not have my talents belittled. I taught her everything, and in precious little time, I'd point out!"

Hattie matched my grin. "That's as may be, but in my turn I'd demand credit for her sharp mind, which is often overlooked in a woman."

I took Hattie's hand from my cheek and kissed it. "And honor—and valor. And many more qualities besides, that I swear I shall not soon forget. Qualities that seem to thrive in womankind, or so I take it."

Hattie cocked her head on her shoulder, her grin softening into one of the most lovely smiles I think it's ever been my pleasure to receive. "Qualities that seem to appear in the most unlikely, unlooked-for places. Even in too-self-absorbed actors occasionally. Now, another matter. What of the genuine Katherine?"

"We have no lingering fear there. Niles assured me that she had been taken into custody and will be held, comfortable but quite *incommunicado*, until such time as our masquerade is complete."

"Good, good. For all that your characterization was probably apt—that she might well have good reason to hate me for the 'sin' of my mother—still I wish her no harm. Surely the misery of her youth, so far from home and family, must entitle her to a measure of sympathy from us."

At last I could but nod and smile at this remarkable woman and her incredible depth of spirit. To be lying there as she was—debased and abused—and to have her care be not for her own situation, but for the comfort of the last child of that family that had so wretchedly used both her and her family—I was again amazed by her.

It was all quite beyond me. Should I be granted another hundred years, I think it highly unlikely that I should attain the worth of this most excellent woman, though through all the years that have come after, I have striven to do so.

We stayed that way for a span of time I cannot now quantify, her hand in mine.

Finally she sighed once more.

"Nathan, I'm weary and you must go. It would not do for 'Katherine' to be found here. I wonder, have we not, perhaps, been a bit too clever for our own good? These new roles we've undertaken—the distance and disdain on your part, and the subservience and dullness on mine—surely we've set demanding characterizations for ourselves now."

"Perhaps, but I can think of none better than us to attempt the performance."

Her smile became wistful. "Perhaps. I wonder what reviews we shall get when the curtain finally falls?"

Finis
Book One

If you liked this story: **Please go to its Amazon page and write a five-star review. Thank you.**